Glass... a wit... fire

Bolan r... ...nd toward the shadowy figure holding the automatic rifle. He grabbed a fistful of Leo Turrin's trench coat and propelled the man toward the elevators. "Go!"

The Executioner changed clips on the run, throwing a quick glance over his shoulder as he raced down the corridor. The assassins wouldn't give up their quarry easily.

Turrin was holding the elevator doors open when Bolan reached the cage. "Take it down, Leo."

"You can't stay up here."

"Get Howell out of the way and call for backup. Somebody's got to stay here and run interference."

Turrin's protests were cut off by the closing doors.

Bolan sprinted to the fire escape, intending to use the heavy metal door as a barricade against the invaders. As he pushed it open, a gunman tumbled through the shattered window and swung his rifle into target acquisition, the Executioner dead in his sights.

MACK BOLAN®

The Executioner

DON PENDLETON'S
THE EXECUTIONER®
FEATURING MACK BOLAN®

ICE WOLF

A GOLD EAGLE BOOK FROM
WORLDWIDE®

TORONTO • NEW YORK • LONDON • PARIS
AMSTERDAM • STOCKHOLM • HAMBURG
ATHENS • MILAN • TOKYO • SYDNEY

First edition November 1989

ISBN 0-373-61131-5

Special thanks and acknowledgment to
Mel Odom for his contribution to this work.

PROLOGUE

The Past

Field Marshal Erwin Rommel raised a hand to his temple, plagued by one of the frequent headaches that were constant reminders of the Livarot attack that had almost killed him. He sought refuge in the garden behind his villa, though by all rights he knew he should be in bed, fast asleep beside Lucce. They had spent the previous day driving and visiting with their longtime friend, Oskar Farny.

Absently he rubbed the indentation in his skull, wondering why the flesh had no feeling whatsoever yet the brain beneath seemed to constantly ache.

The October chill made him shiver under the housecoat, and his breath plumed out before him in the spare moonlight. The doctors he had seen had prescribed painkiller after painkiller to help him get through the worst of it, but Rommel disdained taking them. If the pain was going to be a constant thing with him now, it was going to have to also be something he could master. Alone. By God, there was still a war to be fought, and maybe something to salvage as well if he could get the Führer to listen to reason.

For weeks he had listened to bits and pieces of plots and counterplots about seizing control of the country from Hitler, yet none of them had seemed concrete. Except for the bomb blast in Berlin only a few short weeks ago. The fallout from that episode hadn't been completely sifted through yet.

He stumbled over a rock in the yard, thought about picking it up and discarded the idea almost at once. The headache was bad enough without risking additional agony by bending over.

"General."

The voice drifted softly through the night air, sending chills up Rommel's spine when he identified the speaker. He whirled about, unmindful of the sickening pressure inside his head, his right hand dipping into the housecoat pocket for the Luger he always carried. He leveled the weapon, searching the darkness.

"Put your gun away, General. Had I wanted to kill you, you would have already been dead."

"Von Thoma?" Rommel called in something more than a whisper.

"The same."

A group of shadows twisted to Rommel's left, and he saw the tall man step into blurred reality under a nearby tree. The major's hair seemed white under the moonlight. His eyes were hidden by pools of inky blackness, but Rommel would never forget their wild blue hue. Nor their inhuman coldness. "I could shoot you now for desertion," Rommel said acidly.

"I didn't desert, General."

"I looked for you in the retreat from Montgomery's forces at Alam al-Halfa. You weren't there."

"That's because I didn't retreat." An easy smile touched von Thoma's lips.

Rommel let the pistol drop to his side but didn't put it away. Major Wolfgang von Thoma remained an enigma, even though Rommel's acquaintanceship with the man spanned two years.

"I went into Cairo behind the Britishers' backs," von Thoma explained as he stepped forward.

"You're an SS spy, then?"

"Once, perhaps, General Rommel, but no more. Now I serve the German people. As I hope to get you to."

"I *am* serving the people."

"Are you? Or are you satisfying the whims of the madman who happens to run the country now?"

"Talk like that will get you imprisoned if not killed," Rommel warned.

"I know, but the truth dies slowly. That's why the Führer hastens each departure as it arises."

"What are you doing here tonight?" Rommel looked over his shoulder to make sure his bedroom light was off. Too often Lucce woke while he was trying to relax on one of his midnight walks. It wouldn't do to have her walk up on someone as unstable as he knew von Thoma to be.

"I came to save your life," von Thoma said flatly.

Rommel grinned without mirth. "As you can see, I'm in no danger."

"Yes, you are. Tomorrow Generals Burdorf and Maisel will be arriving at your villa to let you know you have been implicated in conspiracies against Hitler. It's only because our Führer respects you, or more precisely, respects the feelings your name generates in the German populace, that you will be given a choice of suicide over being executed."

The words had the impact of cold nails being driven into Rommel's flesh. The headache became a whirling maelstrom of raw agony. For a while, since the bombing at Berlin, he had been experiencing a feeling of impending doom. "Why should I believe you?"

"Search inside yourself," von Thoma suggested "Why shouldn't you?"

Rommel remained silent, feeling the cold fingers of a bleak future close in around him.

"You're an intelligent man," von Thoma continued after a moment. "You see the writing on the wall. You know this war is over for Germany, but Hitler will never see that. He will push this country until there's nothing left for the German people. There's a new world dawning, and we can be visionaries."

"A Fourth Reich?"

Von Thoma shook his head. "No more Reichs. No more Hitlers. World power will shift after this war. The United States and Russia will be the two big superpowers. France lacks the centralization of government, and Great Britain no longer has the resources to call on. But neither the United States or Russia will be able to trust each other, not until years from now, and by that time my group will be ready to strike."

"And how do you plan to strike?"

"I have wealth and I have people who know how to make that wealth work for me. Already, at my base of operations in Cairo, my money is hard at work earning interest from the war, from munitions and from the alcohol the soldiers drink in the bars."

"All this since you have been there?"

"I have had two years, General. A man can accomplish much in that time if he truly believes in what he wants and really has a passion for it."

"Do you plan to come back to Germany and lead the new war effort?" Rommel asked. The pistol was a leaden weight at the end of his arm.

"No." Von Thoma shifted under the tree. "The uneasiness between the United States and Russia will escalate. Each will wish to dominate world affairs but neither will establish a firm position. I've invested heavily in science and technology as well, General. Diversifying my resources, so to speak. Even in this war we have seen new products and procedures come about. Vulcanized tires, new weapons, rockets, potato gasoline. Science is only now beginning to break its stride."

"You still haven't said how you'll bring about a new era for Germany."

"It may not be for Germany," von Thoma said. "But for the German people, yes, I will establish a way. We are a proud people, a people with history, a people deserving of more honor than the Allies gave us at the end of the last World War, or will give us at the end of this one. But there will be people to lead at the end of it, no matter what they are called a score or more years from now."

Rommel was quiet. For years he had been a devout believer in Hitler's policies. Then he had suddenly realized, too late to save the Afrika Korps, that the country was following a madman. Von Thoma had the same sound in his voice, possessed the same charisma.

"When the United States and Russia are at their weakest," von Thoma continued, "then I will strike quietly, setting them at each other's throat. Then the German people will come into what is rightfully theirs."

Rommel's headache had vanished, and he was surprised to note its absence. "Why do you come to me with this?"

"Because I respect you as a man and as a general. I want you to be with me."

"I have family."

"Bring them with you," von Thoma said. "There's room for all of us. If not in one place, then surely in another. Though I will want to keep you by my side. Your face is too well-known even in the Allied countries to escape detection for long.''

Rommel stared at von Thoma through the shadows, wondering how the man's insanity had managed to capture his interest so well after everything he had gone through with Hitler.

"Will you come with me?" von Thoma entreated.

Rommel shook his head. "I can't. I have sworn to follow Hitler until the end of the war. I have given my word."

"Break your word! Haven't you been listening to what I've said? People are coming here tomorrow to kill you or ask you to kill yourself!"

"You offer a double standard, Major von Thoma," Rommel said with a trace of humor in his voice. "You tell me on one hand that you respect me for being a man of my word, then in the next breath you ask me to break my word. How would you see me if I left now and went with you?"

Von Thoma was silent.

For a moment Rommel thought he had pushed the madman too far, had found some edge for sanity to drop away from. Would the man attempt to kill him if he couldn't be swayed in his decision?

"Perhaps you're right, General. Perhaps we're both trapped by our destinies. Still, if you're able to survive the events of tomorrow, let me know. Escape if you can and come to Cairo, to the main court of the al-Azhar Mosque. Show this device around and someone will help you find me." Von Thoma threw a disk to Rommel.

The general caught it, surprised at its heaviness. Both sides of the solid gold coin showed a stylized bird that appeared to be swimming through the sky rather than flying.

"That's my sigil," von Thoma explained. "And if you look closely, you can see the lines of the swastika."

When Rommel looked up again, he could find no sign of von Thoma. Coldness spread throughout him when he considered the man's dire predictions. Was it true? Could the Führer truly believe him to be guilty of some conspiracy and condemn him to death? The war had taken such unexpected and bloody turns. Even children were fighting as soldiers.

He returned to the house, and his fingers shook as he dialed a telephone number. He had to tell a trusted friend about von Thoma. Someone had to watch out for the man in case his promise of death came true as he said it would. There had been enough war in the world already. More than enough by the time the latest one rolled to its inevitable conclusion. The gold coin felt heavy in his palm as he listened to the line ring on the other end. How many lives would von Thoma's scheme claim in the future? Rommel shuddered to think about it.

1

The Present

Easing the low-slung Pontiac Trans Am through the late-night traffic, Mack Bolan glanced occasionally at the clipboard lying in the passenger seat. He didn't doubt the information the Secret Service teams had put in the report he was following, but he wanted the chance to drive the route for himself. There was too much riding on this meet between Gorbachev and the new President. Not only would it be the Soviet leader's formal introduction to the Man, but it would probably set the tone for the upcoming international summit talks concerning the use of nuclear weapons. The last President had made giant strides in the world peace effort, and people in many countries were waiting to see what would happen now that the teams had changed slightly.

The sports car rolled like a silent shadow down Pennsylvania Avenue, nearing the White House. Bolan mentally checked off the numbers from the printed page Hal Brognola had given him earlier in the day, comparing the estimated times with what he experienced. The big Fed had been tense, irritated, as he told the Executioner about the information the CIA had turned up concerning the Russian's arrival, relaying the vague hints that they'd uncovered about an upcoming assassination attempt.

Nothing definite, Brognola had said, nor even any idea about which country might stage the attempt. The Man himself had asked for Bolan.

He turned off Pennsylvania Avenue onto Seventeenth Street and parked the Trans Am in an outside space near the Renwick Gallery. After powering down the electric windows, he cut the engine.

There had been other threats concerning past visits, Bolan reflected as he watched the D.C. traffic flow through the streets. The Secret Service did a good job as long as the people they were guarding didn't insist on taking too many chances in open areas. With this assignment, they didn't have that luxury. The whole world would be watching.

Bolan believed in the reason behind the summit meetings and didn't want to see the tenuous thrust that had been built between the two countries go down in flames. Especially not here, with the Russians under the protection of the American government. That would serve the purposes of certain Russian factions who were protesting Gorbachev's "westernization" of the USSR and force the wedge already separating the two countries even deeper.

He settled back in the seat, grateful for the plushness of the sports car. He left the radio off, enjoying the silence that surrounded him. For the moment, he had abandoned the role of the hunter. He considered going to the hotel in the downtown area where Brognola had made reservations in the name of Michael Belasko. Maybe later, he told himself, after he'd had a chance to unwind.

The black sports car hugged the shadows in the parking lot, and Bolan was sure he was an almost invisible wraith behind the tinted windows...until the police car pulled off Seventeenth Street and rolled toward him.

The bright headlights of the vehicle splashed across the windshield of the Trans Am, reducing Bolan's vision to an assault of brilliant whiteness. He shifted, letting the lightweight leather jacket he wore slide open enough to allow instant access to the .44 Magnum Desert Eagle and the Beretta 93-R, but not enough to reveal their presence readily.

The police officers' silhouettes looked like two-dimensional cutouts against the brightness of the patrol car's beams.

Bolan narrowed his eyes and looked away from the lights, waiting for his night vision to clear. Chances were this was a legitimate investigation by legitimate cops, but the Executioner didn't rely on chance unless he had exhausted every other avenue. He balanced his weight inside the sports car, preparing to throw himself against the passenger door and roll clear of the vehicle if need arose. It didn't figure that whatever forces were planning the attack on the Soviet leader and the President would know of Bolan's presence. Hell, half of Brognola's team and the Secret Service hadn't seen him in the flesh yet. All they had been privy to so far was the background information Aaron Kurtzman had inserted into the files of the various security groups' computers—and the KGB's.

Bolan watched as one of the policemen stepped to the side of the car with his right hand locked around the butt of his holstered .38. The guy was young, with a baby face and the blocky build of a professional linebacker. He didn't wear a hat, and the hot, dry wind that had risen blew his hair into short-cropped disarray.

"Could I see some identification, sir?"

Reaching out slowly, Bolan handed over the automobile package for the Trans Am that Brognola had given him earlier, as well as his "Belasko" driver's license.

"Keep your hands on the dash, please," the policeman ordered as he walked to the rear of the sports car.

Bolan lifted his hands and kept them in sight, trusting that Kurtzman's magical computers had fully fleshed out the Belasko identity without forgetting to enter the Trans Am's plates and registration in D.C.'s Department of Motor Vehicles. One of the policemen kept an eye on Bolan while the other went back to the patrol car to run the Belasko ID through the police computer.

Then Bolan's car phone rang. "Belasko," he said into the receiver quietly, shifting to monitor the nearest cop's movements in the side mirror.

"Striker?"

Bolan recognized the voice as Leo Turrin's, but the anxiety he heard alarmed him. Turrin had been a Bolan ally from the first bullet fired in Pittsfield, although the Executioner had learned the fact almost too late to keep the guy from becoming a casualty. Turrin had been an up-and-coming young Mafia lord then—as well as an undercover cop for the Justice Department. From time to time, the tightrope Turrin walked between his separate worlds crossed Mack Bolan's path, and in several cases they had stood hard for each other when the chips were down. In the barren soil of the hellgrounds, the friendship had flowered. Like Bolan, Turrin had adopted many names and still had access to more than a few. The latest was as department head Leonard Justice, operating out of Justice.

"Go ahead, Leo," Bolan said softly so that his voice wouldn't carry past the receiver. In the rearview mirror he saw the first cop, the one who had spoken to him, bend forward for a moment and flick on his flashlight to scan the sports car's plates. When the big man reached out to touch the car, Bolan's warning senses buzzed loudly.

"I didn't want to call you over an open channel," Turrin said, "but I need your help and I don't have a lot of time."

"Where are you?"

Turrin gave him the address. "I don't know what we're facing here, Striker, but it involves some pretty heavy hitters. From what I've turned up, at least a dozen people have been executed in the past ten or twelve days. I've asked enough right questions in the wrong places that somebody's probably made me by now." He sighed heavily. "I feel guilty every time I call Angelina. I haven't seen her in five days because I've been trying to move on this thing quickly and quietly. She thought all the undercover-in-the-field stuff was over. Hell, so did I."

"Give me fifteen or twenty minutes," Bolan said, cutting into Turrin's monologue smoothly. He could almost feel the exhaustion in the man through the connection. Turrin had always maintained a sense of humor in situations where life seemed to hang on every heartbeat. It wasn't danger that was wearing on the little Fed now, the warrior knew, but something definitely was.

"Be careful coming in, big guy," Turrin warned. "Like I said, the team we're hunting probably has my number and I haven't got a damn thing on them. But they're definitely unfriendlies."

Bolan said goodbye and replaced the receiver as the first police officer approached the door. The Executioner accepted the papers from the man and returned the grin he was given.

"Sorry to detain you, Mr. Belasko," the officer said, "but it made me kind of edgy to see you sitting back in here so quietly."

"I've been moving around a lot these past few days," Bolan explained as he tossed the papers on top of the clipboard. "I found out I was more tired than I thought and figured I'd clear my head for a few minutes before I tried to make it back to my hotel."

The cop nodded affably and walked back to the cruiser, joining his partner. He climbed in and started the engine, pulling forward to give Bolan a final wave before easing back into traffic.

Bolan waited until the vehicle faded from view, then got out of the car. He took a penlight from a shirt pocket and squatted behind the rear bumper. Alternately using his eyes and his fingertips, he searched the back of the Trans Am, grunting in satisfaction when he found the magnetic tracer locked to the undercarriage of the car. He turned it over in his hands, trying to figure out if it was domestic or foreign.

The cops, if the guys really were police officers, had definitely been looking for him tonight. But were they operating on their own, or were they part of a team assembled to find out who Michael Belasko was? CIA, FBI or KGB? he wondered. Or part of the group setting up the assassination strike?

Bolan closed his eyes and drew in a breath, letting it out slowly. He pictured the cruiser in his mind, watching it roll out of the parking area again, this time at his command. Mentally he froze the cruiser at a time when the glow of the surrounding streetlights had lit up the plates. He concentrated on the numbers, then locked them into his memory. Kurtzman could unravel whatever trail accompanied the "cops" and the car. Right now Leo needed him.

He dropped the bug onto the pavement, thinking whoever was trying to monitor his activities might conclude the device had vibrated loose on its own. It would at least give him a few minutes to lose himself before someone noticed the vehicle wasn't moving.

He fastened his seat belt and jammed the Desert Eagle beside the passenger seat so that he could get to it quickly, then kicked the engine over and slid the car into gear.

BOLAN HAD NO DIFFICULTY finding the address Turrin had given him. He guided the sports car through the quiet streets, seeing reflections of the Trans Am's lights mirrored in blackened department store and office windows. He flicked down the window and looked up at the building Turrin had singled out.

It was an older structure that had been refurbished during the urban renewal effort of the fifties and sixties. Standing ten stories high, it was dwarfed by most of the other buildings around it. D.C. hadn't started going upward with the increasing community until much later.

Bolan parked the car at the curb and walked to the corner coffee shop where Leo had said he would be. His heels rang hollowly on the pavement, and he hunkered his shoulders against the light rain that had started falling moments earlier.

He darted a quick glance at the office building again, trying to fathom why Turrin would be there. Brognola had mentioned the little Fed's absence in passing but hadn't seemed concerned about it. Evidently Turrin hadn't been checking in regularly. Or maybe not at all. The realization that something might have happened to Leo during the time it had taken him to drive across the city made Bolan's guts twist. He forced himself to keep his steps calm and measured despite the feeling of helplessness that gripped him.

A shadow separated itself from the gloom in front of the small coffee shop and walked toward Bolan.

The Executioner moved in closer to the wall beside him. He felt his heartbeat surge and felt the fatigue drop away from him, suppressed by his internal survival mechanism.

The shadow wore an unfamiliar slouch hat and olive trench coat, but the gait belonged to Leo Turrin. The man from Justice lifted his hands and showed Bolan the coffee cups he was carrying.

Bolan fell into step behind Turrin as the man led the way to the darkened doorway of a printing shop that conducted business only during daylight hours.

"If I'm going to keep you up tonight," Turrin said, "the least I can do is buy you a cup of coffee."

Bolan broke the perforation and smelled the liquid, feeling his taste buds kick into overdrive. How long had it been since he'd eaten? He couldn't honestly remember. There had been too much to absorb today with Brognola and the security teams.

"What's on tap, Leo?" Bolan asked. He noticed the heavy bags under the man's eyes in the dim light of the streetlights, as well as the slouch of his friend's shoulders. Turrin had been pursuing his objective for some time, he realized, and wondered why something so important couldn't be taken to Brognola.

"Have you been stateside for the past few days, Sarge?"

Bolan shook his head.

Turrin took a big gulp of coffee, scowling at the sudden furnace heat of it. "I can't even taste the damn stuff anymore, I've been drinking it so long." He sighed heavily. "You knew I was involved in the Witness Protection Program?"

"I'd heard."

"As Leonard Justice, I've supervised a few cases where
we transplanted whole families to new locations and new
identities. So I keep my hand in the program, enrolling
new people and occasionally checking up on old ac-
quaintances. Two weeks ago a guy turned up dead—
someone I helped drop out of sight after he put the finger on a gambling operation under Vito Scorscini in
Pittsfield a year or so before—" he hesitated over his
choice of words, then shrugged and went on "—before
you got back from Nam. Him, his wife and three sons.
All of them were executed with a shotgun."

Bolan heard the break in Turrin's voice but didn't say
anything, knowing it was a pain the man would have to
work out on his own.

"The guy had been relocated here in D.C.," Turrin
went on after a moment. "He was bright, Mack. A real
family man. I envied him that. He always talked about
his boys and how they were doing in sports, about how
he and his wife always made time to go to their games, no
matter how confused their schedules got. I only got to
talk to him three, maybe four times, to let him know what
was going on. I felt responsible for the guy. I was the one
who convinced him to help put Scorscini away."

"He must have been put away pretty deep to have been
under this long, Leo."

Turrin nodded. "Not deep enough, though." He
sipped more coffee and stared blankly ahead. "A day or
two later, hell, I can't really remember how all of this
came together anymore, I found out another family in the
program was murdered here in the D.C. area. A lady who
had testified in a rape case against one of the Five Families' top dogs in New York. One of the don's favorite
nephews or something. The guy went to prison and got

killed in a fight. By that time the Feds had her and her daughter spirited away. After I found this out, I started looking, Mack. Really looking. You know how it is when you know you know something but can't really put your finger on what is it you know?''

Bolan nodded tightly, sensing the frustration and torment Turrin was trying to hold back.

"I spent two days poring over murder files here in Washington, branching out into the suburbs. I took files home at night and locked myself away from Angelina and the kids. God, I owe that woman a week out on the town after this is over with. I haven't been able to tell her where I was day after day because I was afraid someone would be monitoring my phone. I've found bugs in my house before, goddamn it, put there by the CIA, the FBI, God knows who else. Not very often, maybe, but enough to let me know guys on our side don't really trust the fact that my association with the Mafia was strictly undercover work.''

"So what did you find?" Bolan asked, watching Turrin slump against the brick wall. The trench coat had slid open and exposed the Smith & Wesson .38 Bodyguard he had holstered butt-forward on his left hip. Leo hadn't been one much for guns, and Bolan wondered what it was that made his friend feel so vulnerable. Or so protective.

"Twelve people, Mack," the little Fed stated in a cold and neutral voice Bolan wouldn't have recognized if he hadn't heard it coming from the man's lips. "In the past two weeks twelve people living in D.C. under the Witness Protection Program have been killed. Nobody knows about it or even seems to have correlated the deaths. Except me."

"Because you were looking for it."

Turrin nodded. "These people were placed in the city by different groups associated with the program, so it may take some time for the information to filter back to the main office. Even longer before the connection is made. In the meantime, more people are going to die."

"You think someone inside the program is dirty?" The thought turned Bolan's stomach cold and hard inside. It had taken a lot of bravery for the witnesses to testify in court, and those individuals had known the price they were going to have to pay for that bravery. They had been ripped from familiar settings and placed in sometimes strange and new environments, where they could trust no one and had to carefully keep in mind the manufactured pasts the government agencies had given them. And all this while they were the innocent ones.

"Damn it, Mack, I don't know what to think. These people are getting their information from somewhere."

"What people?"

"I guess I'm getting a little ahead of myself." Turrin drained the rest of his coffee. "After I put all this together, I hit the bricks myself. Most of the police agencies in town are tied up with planning the meet between Gorbachev and the new Prez. And I didn't have a lot to go on. Sure, four different families in the program have been wiped out, but the statistics in this town for murder are high enough that maybe that fact wouldn't throw a red flag out to anyone. Maybe I was taking it too personal. At any rate, I still have connections in a few of the right places. Quiet connections, though."

Bolan switched to a different quadrant of the star-filled sky as helicopter rotors tore through the night. He located the source of the churning engines as it blew in from the east with the dry wind.

"A guy who would know told me Scorscini was contacted by a group offering to put the witness and his family down for a price. The amount was right, my guy said, and Scorscini put it up."

"Did you get a name?" Bolan asked.

Turrin shook his head. "I don't know if Scorscini got one. My guy said the leader of the group gave Scorscini some pictures of another family they had done. It convinced Scorscini."

"And he was interested after all these years?"

"Yeah, you know how it is with the Families, Mack. An eye for an eye as long as both parties live."

"What brings you here?"

Turrin pointed at the office building across the street. "This is where the next hit is supposed to take place."

"How sure are you?" Bolan shifted, scanning the almost deserted street. Overhead the helicopter was making another pass.

"Sure enough to call you once I pried the number out of Brognola."

"What did you tell Hal?"

"That I had a hunch about some things and wanted a backup. He agreed that you were the one to call. I don't want anyone else on it yet, Mack. There'd be too much clutter around us to be able to get a fix on this thing."

Bolan nodded. He had already been feeling the pressure of too many teams working on one project with the surveillance concerning the arrival of the Soviets. It felt good to be moving again on his own, with no restrictions and no laws except the ones he lived and fought by. "Who's in the building?"

Turrin joined him at the front of the doorway. "Kirby Howell. He's a lawyer working for a small firm on the eighth floor. Wednesday nights are his night to stay late and do the files." Turrin checked his watch. "It's almost ten now. He should be finishing soon."

Bolan studied the lights on the eighth floor, watching to see how much of the room was visible to the outside observer. There were no curtains that he could see, but none of the nearby buildings were high enough to allow a sniper beyond the building's perimeter. The assassination would have to take place inside. "Does Howell know?"

"Yeah, I contacted him a couple of hours ago before I started trying to find you. He agreed to stay at work until I could get him an escort home. I've already assigned four agents to protect his son."

"It takes a pretty gutsy guy to sit there knowing someone is stalking him."

"Howell *is* a gutsy guy," Turrin replied. "He's in his early thirties and grew up in Harlem. He was good at track and got a scholarship to go to college. Then he held down a couple of nighttime jobs while he earned his law degree. Three years ago, he saw Adelio Madrano personally execute one of his rivals in the street and testified at the trial. At first he refused protection from the program, believing everything had been settled in court. He came home one evening to find two men torching his apartment. Howell broke the door down and forced his way through the flames. He managed to save his three-year-old son, but his wife was dead. Six months later the program shuffled him here."

"You're sure the hit is supposed to go down tonight?"

"Madrano's father was promised, and you don't give a promise to someone of his rank lightly."

"You might if you were sure no one knew who you were."

"Yeah," Turrin agreed, "but these guys have a proven track record they're using to promote their business."

"It sounds like they know the whole setup before they ever approach their buyers. They just lay the scenario out and name their price."

Turrin nodded.

Bolan glanced at his watch. Ten o'clock. "How many people are in the building?"

"Maybe twenty, including the four security people, and most of those are scattered over all ten floors."

"It's time for Howell to check out, isn't it?"

"Yeah."

As he led the way across the street, Bolan checked his weapons. The Desert Eagle and Beretta were familiar weights across his upper body. His jacket pockets contained two garrotes and a short knife. The Gerber combat blade was sheathed upside down on his right calf for an easier draw.

He let Turrin take the lead when they reached the first security checkpoint and watched him show the guard his Justice ID. Just as Bolan stepped inside the air-conditioned atmosphere of the building, he heard the chopper rotors pass by again. Then the door closed and he had his own ID out for inspection.

"Thanks for coming, Mack."

"You've been there for me."

A feeling of lightness in Bolan's stomach signaled their arrival at the eighth floor. The doors slid back. The Executioner checked Leo's movement with a hand and held the door open, sweeping the empty hallway with a glance before they stepped out.

Canned music followed them down the tiled hallway as they made their way to Howell's office. The Executioner surveyed the closed doors of the three other offices on the floor, ready to move quickly if he had to.

Turrin knocked and waited.

Bolan could see the tension eating at the smaller man in the way Turrin kept balling his fists as he stood before the door and tried to look unconcerned. When the little Fed raised his hand to knock again, the door opened.

The black man behind the door glanced at Bolan, but didn't step back to admit either man. He was young, Bolan saw, and looked like he belonged in the three-piece suit he wore. The only thing that looked out of place was the automatic filling his right hand and the worried look that mirrored Turrin's.

"This the guy you were telling me about, Leo?" Howell asked.

"Yeah. Any problems?"

The man shook his head.

Flashing lights drew Bolan's attention away from Howell. He stared at the window at the end of the hall, past the blackness of the heavy tint, and saw lights suspended eight stories up just as the vibration from the helicopter's rotors echoed in his ears.

The glass shattered under a sudden burst of autofire, fragments skittering brightly across the tiled floor like diamonds.

Bolan unleathered the .44 smoothly and drilled a 240-grain hollowpoint toward the shadowy figure holding the automatic rifle. He grabbed a fistful of Turrin's trench coat and pulled him toward the elevators, realizing the office was no place to be trapped. "Follow Leo," the Executioner growled at Howell. He held the Magnum in a Weaver's grip and finished off the 8-round clip into the side of the helicopter, watching the chopper rise out of view.

He changed clips on the run, keeping watch over his shoulder, knowing the attackers wouldn't give up easily.

Turrin was holding the elevator doors open when Bolan reached the cage, the .38 S&W Bodyguard in his right hand. Howell had his own weapon up and ready.

"Take it down, Leo," Bolan directed as he punched the first floor.

"You can't stay up here," Turrin protested.

"Get Howell out of the way," Bolan said as the doors closed, "and call for some backup. Somebody's got to stay here and run interference."

Turrin's words were cut off by the closing doors.

Bolan double-timed it to the fire escape, intending to use the heavy metal door as a barricade against the invaders. As he pushed it open, a man tumbled through the shattered window and fell into a prone position, dropping his rifle into target acquisition.

2

Autofire raced down the hallway, drumming a rapid tattoo against the metal skin of the fire escape door.

Bolan gripped the doorframe and threw himsel around the corner, coming to a halt with his back pressed against the wall, the Desert Eagle held against his ear Torn metal stuck out from the door where rounds hac chewed into it.

Residual heat from outside the building choked the narrow spiral of the fire escape, and Bolan could feel hi shirt sticking to his back. How many men were there? And how the hell had this hit become so important? Somebody with dirty hands in the Witness Protection Program he could buy, but not this. Whoever was putting the assassination teams together wasn't assembling them with halfway measures.

He yanked the fire escape door open, whirling back as more bullets whined off the concrete wall across from him. The brief glance he had been allowed showed him two more men had joined the battle.

The warrior pushed off the wall and headed down the steel-reinforced steps. His booted feet clumped noisily in the emptiness of the emergency exit. He bounced off the first wall at the bottom of the initial flight of stairs, placing a big palm on the yellow 7 painted there, in order to help change the direction of his momentum.

He kept expecting to hear the door above him explode open as the assassins pursued him.

Had they seen Turrin and Howell board the elevator? Or had they assumed the man they were after had preceded him into the fire exit? They would check the elevators, he told himself, and would notice the descending cage. They wouldn't let the possibility that their quarry was inside the elevator go unchecked. This was strictly a military operation, a seek-and-strike mission that would leave only scorched earth in its wake.

It was possible that they had someone waiting on the bottom floor and that he had sent Leo straight into their sights.

Damning himself for not thinking the situation through before punching the button, Bolan pulled the door open and stepped out onto the seventh floor. For a moment he was lost in the darkness that filled the corridor. His eyes darted to the glowing yellow numbers over the elevator farthest from him, wondering if Leo was safe.

The elevator nearest him was in motion now, too, dropping only a handful of floors behind the little Fed's, leaving the fire escape as the only route down.

The only conventional route, Bolan corrected himself as he ran to the last office on the left at the end of the hall. Clenching the Desert Eagle in both hands, he raised his right foot and smashed it into the door beside the locking mechanism. The entrance gave with a metallic screech as screws and bolt pulled through the soft wooden frame. The force of the kick knocked the big door backward, stabbing the knob into the plaster wall.

Movement behind Bolan alerted him to the fact that he wasn't alone. He dropped to one knee, taking advantage of the partial security offered by the open door as he leveled the .44, cupping the Magnum's butt in his left palm.

The warrior used his peripheral vision to penetrate the gloom. Three men, he figured. Two on the right and one on the left. How many men did that leave pursuing Turrin and Howell? He pushed the question out of his mind. There wasn't enough intel to go on yet. Too damn many for sure.

"Where the hell is he?" The disembodied whisper drifted down the hallway, and Bolan couldn't be sure which man had spoken.

"I don't know."

A Klaxon sounded without warning, filling the floor with a roar of noise as emergency lights flared to life. The sound of a muffled explosion came from above.

Startled, Bolan glanced at the lighted numbers above the elevator shaft, watching it wink out weakly while signaling the third floor. Then he was hunting cover as the three men opened fire, falling back into the office as splinters gouged for his flesh.

Dropping to the floor, Bolan fisted the .44 in his left hand and crawled to the doorway again. He kept his hand and arm behind him as he peered around the violated doorframe, then swung the big handcannon into target acquisition as one of his attackers sprinted for the office.

Bolan waited until the guy was opposite the door, wanting to be sure of putting at least one of them away. The emergency lights in the corners of the hallway gave him a brief glimpse of the dark uniform the gunner wore. The man's face seemed disjointed under the illusion of the combat cosmetic he wore, as if different faces had contributed to the composition of this one, the pieces arranged clumsily.

The warrior aimed the big Magnum, unloading a pair of .44 skullbusters at the center of the Halloween face, watching it dissolve before the sudden high-powered onslaught. The man's body was blown backward against the opposite wall, the body leaving a dark, oily smear as it sank to the floor.

Bolan was up and mobile again before the corpse finished its slide. He was sure the outside team had blown the generators, plunging the building into semidarkness and perhaps trapping Turrin and Howell between floors in the elevator. He kept the .44 up and ready and threaded his way through the office. He found the inner office door and hurried through.

Once inside the small office, Bolan closed the door behind him. Taking the penlight from inside his jacket, he thumbed it on and scanned the room. Lurid posters of exotic locations with shapely, tanned flesh leaped out at him, grabbing his attention for a moment. Then he turned his eyes to the office phone, tracing the length of phone cord trailing from the box.

He holstered the Desert Eagle and focused on the cord. Using a small pocketknife, he cut the phone cord and started to pull on it, following its length to the base of the wall. Staples popped free of the wood and fell onto the carpet.

He strained to hear whatever noise the men might make as they approached the inner office, waiting expectantly for a scuff or scrape, wondering if any movement would be audible in the closeness of the room. Already the air was turning stale and muggy, unable to be released through the air-conditioning and backup air units.

The phone cord came free easily, and he twisted it over his palm and under his elbow as he gathered it. How

many feet could he get? For a moment it became stuck
under the inner door. His shoulder and back muscles
strained as he pulled on it with both hands. It held long
enough for muscle cramps to start, then popped loose,
the end of the cord snapping against the door.

Before the small echo could die away, a burst of slugs
thudded through the shallow wooden paneling of the
door, ripping from top to bottom without pause.

Bolan spun away, unlimbering the .44 and triggering
off three rounds that made holes he could put his fist
through. Then he was at the window, lifting the phone in
his fist and swinging it at the glass. The first blow left
spiderwebbed cracks that ran from top to bottom. The
second emptied the frame of most of the glass, and he
used the butt of his gun to remove the rest of it.

He looked down at the street seven floors below, then
back at the shattered door, realizing he had no choice. He
had been in tighter situations, he told himself as he secured one end of the phone cord to the desk, but he was
damned if he could remember one at the moment.

Thinking of Leo trapped in the stalled elevator with the
remainder of the hit squad working its way down to him,
Bolan threw a leg out of the window, letting his body
follow naturally. Under his weight, the desk scooted
jerkily across the carpet until it came to a stop against the
wall below the window. After testing the knot he'd made
in the slim wire, the warrior grabbed twin fistfuls of the
doubled strand and rappeled downward, working his way
slowly to the window below on the next floor.

Whirling rotors screamed around the building toward
his position. Realizing he'd be visible to the chopper pilot, Bolan kicked away from the building, letting the cord
slide through his hands with almost burning speed. The
aircraft turned the near corner of the building with

agonizing slowness, looking like some impossible insect monster from a 1950s science fiction movie.

Bolan turned a half circle as he swung back toward the building, momentarily out of control. He slammed against the brick wall on his right foot, trying to regain control of his momentum. The impact numbed his foot, but needles of returning feeling assaulted it almost immediately, probing just beneath the skin. He saw the helicopter turn on one side, heard the change in the rotor's pitch, then watched it swerve toward him. A rifle barrel protruded from the passenger side of the aircraft.

Bolan propelled himself away from the building, slipping the cord through his hands, aware that the length was approaching the end, hoping it was enough. Bullets whined off the bricks, chipping splinters from his previous position.

The warrior's outward swing took him almost eight feet from the building, then he was penduluming back. Too damn fast, he thought. Yellow muzzle-flashes ignited the darkness to his right and behind him. He wondered briefly why he couldn't hear the sound of the shots. Then he felt the barrier of glass contact his boots, felt enough tautness to wonder if it would give, if he had judged the angle right or if he would only hit a glancing blow and hang suspended from the too-short cord while the gunner on the helicopter picked him off.

He crashed into the glass and exploded through. Curled into a ball at the base of the window, he reached for the Beretta, knowing it held a full clip while the .44 was down to a few rounds.

The helicopter's shadow fell across the window. The Executioner raised himself to a kneeling position, arms stretched outward over the glass-covered ledge. The

Beretta popped as Bolan emptied the clip, his hands shaking as if he'd grabbed hold of an invisible wind.

Even as the 93-R blew back into the locked and empty position, the helicopter gave a full-throated roar and bounded skyward. The chopper was gone before he had a chance to ram another clip into his gun.

Bolan pushed a fresh clip into the Desert Eagle, then unlocked the door of the office he was in and headed for the sixth-floor corridor.

He waited a moment at the outer door before exposing himself. The emergency lights illuminated the hallway with an eerie glow, and the shadows seemed suspended and stretched out across the walls. Seeing no one, he ran for the elevator shaft that Leo and Howell had descended. He shoved the fingers of his right hand through the sliding doors, and they parted grudgingly.

Using the powerful penlight, the Executioner scanned the cavity as best he could. The cage hung suspended two and a half stories below, stranded between two floors.

Bolan leathered the .44 and removed his jacket. Holding it in both hands, he leaped for the elevator cables, feeling the muscle-burning strain tear at his upper body as he fought gravity. He slid down the cable too fast at first, then clamped his hands tighter. His descent slowed as the cable rasped only bare inches from his unprotected face, shredding the jacket.

The impact was considerable, and he went to his knees with the force of it. Bolan located the emergency access panel and used the Gerber to pry it up and remove it.

He didn't look inside. Ignoring the pain in his hand, he wrapped his fingers around the butt of the .44 and tugged it free. He called Leo's name softly.

"Striker?"

Bolan grinned despite the situation. "Yeah." He peered inside the cage, seeing Turrin and Howell pressed against the walls. The faces of both men looked bleak in the lancing beam of the penlight. Shards of glass at Turrin's feet told Bolan the Fed had smashed the interior emergency light to maintain the protection of darkness.

"Give me an arm up," Leo said.

Bolan did, powering the smaller man through the hatch with little difficulty. Then he reached for Howell. Perspiration made his hand slick, and Howell's hand slipped away. He reached again, closing his fingers around the man's wrist. As he pulled, an invasion of light near the man's feet signaled the arrival of the attackers. A rifle barrel moved into the inches-wide opening provided by the doors of the lower floor.

Cursing, Bolan yanked with everything he had, knowing if the gunner sprayed the interior of the elevator, the ricochets would cut Howell to bloody rags. Thunder erupted inside the cage as the man cleared the opening. Howell gave a muffled groan, and the Executioner recognized the too-familiar sound of a bullet striking flesh.

"Help him, Leo," Bolan growled as he drew the .44. "He caught one." The Desert Eagle drummed a death-beat as he touched off the rounds, knowing they would chew through the thin walls of the elevator into the flesh beyond.

The rifle drew back instantly.

"How bad is it?" Bolan asked as he shoved a fresh clip home. He sensed Leo helping Howell up behind him. The elevator doors to the fourth floor were almost beyond reach.

"Clean one, Mack. In and out the calf."

Bolan glanced over his shoulder, noting the grayness of Howell's face. "Can you make it?"

The man flashed a brief smile. "I got a choice?"

Bolan gave him the ghost of a grin. "If you want to call it that." Leo produced a handkerchief and wrapped it around Howell's leg.

Using the heavy blade of the Gerber to separate the doors over his head, Bolan forced a handhold and levered himself up, widening it as he went. He reached back into the elevator shaft for Howell, helping the man scramble to solid ground.

A hollow thump sounded in the elevator cage as Bolan grabbed Turrin's hand. The sudden widening of Leo's eyes told the Executioner he knew as well as Bolan did what the noise signified. He pulled hard, trying to get his friend up as quickly as possible, feeling their hands slip for one sickening moment. Then Leo was up, rolling onto the carpet away from the shaft.

The whump of the compressed explosion blew the elevator doors from their tracks, one of them smashing heavily against Bolan's legs.

"Get up," the warrior commanded as he pushed himself to his feet. He stood guard while the two men composed themselves, anxious to be moving again. Howell favored his left leg and Turrin stood unsteadily, the trench coat hanging limply.

"Once we reach street level," Bolan said, "we're going to be okay. There are places to hide, to maneuver. Until then, we've got one way down and that's the fire escape. Part of the team that's hunting us will be covering that from below, and you can bet that more of them are in the upper stories."

"Why don't we try to wait them out?" Howell suggested. "Surely the police are on their way."

Bolan shook his head. "They're not playing a waiting game. They came here to get you, and they won't leave until you're dead or become totally inaccessible to them."

Howell's face tightened. "Then leave me here. I'll take my chances until the police come. Maybe they'll let you and Leo go."

"That's not the way these guys operate," Turrin replied. "First they'll kill *you*, then they'll want your son dead. Every time this team operates, it's an all-or-nothing mission. You're the only person I know who's lived through one of their assaults. I've asked enough questions these past two weeks that I can be fairly certain they know me well enough to want me out of the way, too. Chances are they waited until I was in the building before they made their move. What they couldn't count on was the backup we would have with us."

Howell nodded, and the grin he gave Bolan and Turrin was without mirth. "Fair enough, gents. You had your chance to get rid of me."

Bolan took the lead, followed by Howell. Turrin brought up the rear. The warrior cautiously pushed the fire escape door open. Nothing moved. The emergency lights were bright flares at every deck, almost powerful enough to penetrate the darkness gathered like fog around the spiraling stairways.

Aware that he was no longer a single target and had more than just himself to consider, Bolan moved down the first flight of stairs, pressing himself back against the recesses of the wall. He motioned the two men following him onward.

He heard Howell suck in his breath and hold it as they neared the third-floor landing. He wanted to tell the man that not breathing was the last thing his body needed to deal with. Bolan kept his own oxygen flow even and unhurried, at one with the weapons in his hands and with the blood coursing at breakneck pace through his veins.

When he reached the landing, Bolan blocked the door with his foot, standing clear of the entrance in case the gunners tried to shoot their way through. Once Howell and Turrin had cleared the landing, he pulled the door open, flattening himself against the doorframe as he brought up the .44.

The empty hallway gaped back at him. Only the exploded doors of the elevator shaft seemed out of place. Where were they?

The flat crack of Turrin's .38 signaled a fusillade of return fire. The 5.56 mm tumblers splatted against the concrete walls from above, sending sparks shooting across the landing. The gunfire, amplified inside the enclosure, became a dirge from hell that made conversation impossible.

With his forearm, Bolan shoved Howell ahead of him, down the stairs under the temporary safety of the stairway. The warrior slipped the 93-R inside his waistband and grabbed a fistful of Turrin's trench coat, muscling the little Fed over the railing that separated the upper and lower staircases just as a barrage ignited the ironwork into a short-lived fireworks display.

Then Bolan was leading the charge down the final flights of stairs, weapons in both hands.

The bottom door of the fire escape had a small window. Dodging to one side, Bolan tried to penetrate the darkness that lay gathered inside the foyer. He summoned a mental image of how the room had looked when he and Turrin had entered the building earlier—the main desk there, the security office here, artificial plants lining that wall. Then he realized the emergency lights weren't on in the foyer.

Meaning someone was waiting for them to walk through the door. But how many men?

"Sarge?"

"It's a sucker play," Bolan replied, turning his attention to an abandoned garbage bin that stood against the opposite wall. He snared it, noting the pile of crumpled paper inside with grim satisfaction.

Voices, unclear and indistinguishable, drifted down the staircases.

The Executioner removed a matchbook from a jacket pocket, lit the entire book at once and watched as the sheets of paper he held in one hand caught fire with agonizing slowness. Then he tossed them into the bin and fanned the flames into roaring life.

He wheeled the garbage container into position, fisted the Desert Eagle and opened the door. Scanning his companion's faces, he noted the determination lining their jaws.

Bolan lashed out with his foot, and the container resembled a large, barrel-shaped torch as it sped across the darkened foyer. The fire caught greedily, spreading quickly. Then the bin capsized, spilling the flaming contents across the tiled floor and sending unsteady shadows scattering over the walls and ceiling.

Autofire drummed into the receptacle, which seemed to assume a mystical life as the rounds thudded into it, jerking indecisively over the tiles.

Three men were revealed in the uncertain glow from the scattered flames in a strobe effect, centered by the muzzle-flashes of their assault rifles.

Bolan stepped into the doorway of the fire escape and tracked the .44 into target acquisition. He triggered two shots into the chest of the gunner to his left, not waiting to see the corpse fall, knowing the bullets had taken the man in the throat or face. Sweeping on to the second man, he delivered a trio of rounds that punched gaping holes in the guy's torso.

The warrior dived to the floor and rolled under the sudden blast of tumblers that ate away at the wall behind him. A burning paper singed his left cheek as he sighted down the length of the Desert Eagle and squeezed off a round that took off the top of the last gunner's head. The assault rifle clattered to the floor.

Howell and Turrin were on his heels as he scooped the rifle up, identifying it by feel and balance as an AK-47. He freed the clip and found that twelve rounds were left. Two more full clips were on the dead man's web belt, and he helped himself.

Bolan halted again at the entranceway, breathing quickly with the past exertion. A dead security guard slumped over the main desk, a dark stain running down the front of his uniform.

"Son of a bitch," Howell said softly as he stared at the carnage. "Why would they try this hard to get to me?"

Bolan shook his head. He didn't know, either, but he figured he was damn sure going to try to find out. A dozen innocent lives had been snuffed out by killers like the ones whose corpses he'd left behind. Against the sophisticated weaponry those men had carried, and against their fanaticism, the victims had never had a chance. There would be a reckoning, he promised himself.

The street was deserted except for the occasional passing car, but Bolan was aware of the havoc one well-placed sniper could wreak. He looked at Howell and Turrin. "When we get outside, stick close to the building. It will make it harder for someone to pick us off without exposing himself."

Both men nodded their understanding, lifting their weapons as they readied themselves for an all-or-nothing effort.

Bolan pushed the double glass doors open and stepped through, aware of a fleeting movement to his right. Bullets smashed into the building's brick exterior, creating an uneven scar as they searched for Bolan with 5.56 mm talons.

The Executioner whirled back within the safety of the entranceway as the sustained burst chopped through the thin panes of the glass door.

"Shit," Turrin muttered as he forced himself into position by Bolan.

The keening whine of police sirens reached Bolan's ears. Then the dull roar of helicopter rotors settled toward the street from above. Cars approaching from both ends of the street braked to screeching halts as they saw the chopper hovering less than ten feet above the pavement. Automatic rifles blatted to life and caused the drivers to slam their vehicles into reverse.

Bolan noted the rope ladder swinging free beneath the helicopter's chassis and figured the aircraft was making a last pickup run before fleeing the area. A handful of silhouettes filled the cargo bay of the chopper, and the Executioner guessed the team on the upper floors had already made their escape.

Bringing the AK-47 to bear, Bolan emptied the clip, sending the assassins scrambling for cover. When the helicopter powered up and rose away from street level, he turned his attention to the man remaining behind. "Cover me," Bolan shouted as he fed a new clip into the rifle and handed it to Turrin.

"Watch your ass, Mack."

"I want this guy alive, Leo," Bolan said as he reloaded the Desert Eagle. "Maybe he can give us an angle on this operation."

The little Fed grimaced. "If he comes too close, I'm taking him out and you can bitch at me all you want."

Bolan nodded and sprinted for the street, intending to draw the assassin's fire, while Turrin set himself up to drive the guy back under cover.

Bullets bounced and spun from the street, still yards from their target.

Bolan heard Turrin squeeze his own weapon into life as he dived behind the parked Trans Am. Turrin emptied the clip while the Executioner slid into the sports car and hit the ignition. The engine caught smoothly. Holding the .44 in one hand, he stabbed the transmission into low gear and popped the clutch. The back end of the Pontiac powerhouse fishtailed as the tires screamed for traction, cutting a tight one-eighty as Bolan guided the vehicle toward the man hugging the exterior of the office building. A quick glance up showed him the retreating lights of the helicopter.

Bolan hit the brake and double-clutched, swinging the Trans Am in a sideways skid that presented the passenger side of the sports car to the gunner. A burst of 5.56 mm stingers smacked into the side of the car, emptying the windows of safety glass as Bolan dived out the driver's side. He rolled toward the front of the vehicle, gripping the .44 in his right hand as he came up beside the front fender.

Hand, arm and eye cleared the hood of the Trans Am at the same moment. Target acquisition was sought, found.

With the sights hovered on the gunner's right shoulder, Bolan squeezed. He watched the man spin wildly, dropping the AK-47. Remarkably the assassin regained his feet faster than Bolan expected, breaking into a run even as the Executioner slid across the hood of his vehicle. The man's right arm dangled uselessly at his side as he fled.

"Stop," Bolan ordered as he reached the sidewalk and dropped into target stance. The fleeing man's head and shoulders wavered over the top of the Desert Eagle's open sights, but he never missed a staggering step.

Cursing, Bolan fell into cadence behind the man, holding the .44 loose at his side as he ran. He tried to keep the gun close to his body, not wanting to panic any citizens who'd be gathering to find out what was going on.

Pushing himself, Bolan tried to narrow the thirty-yard lead the man maintained on him, surprised at the guy's reserves. It was an adrenaline rush, Bolan told himself as he sucked in fresh oxygen through his nose, exhaling it through his mouth. It had to give out in moments.

Without warning, the man cut to his left, crossing the street, angling for the doorway of a video game arcade where a small crowd of teenagers stood staring. They parted before the fleeing man, staring at the blood-stained fingers that clutched his injured shoulder.

Bolan read hate in their eyes as he charged toward the youths, knowing they assumed he was a cop. He had to turn sideways to wedge through them, listening to the rise of the crowd's antagonistic murmur. A kid in his twenties reached for Bolan's gun hand.

Without breaking stride, the warrior raised an elbow and slammed it into the young man's chin, knocking him back into the crowd.

"Fuckin' pig!" someone yelled.

There was more screaming as other voices joined the first, but Bolan ignored it. He ran through the noisy and flashing video games like a fullback working a busted play.

He found the assassin clawing at the back door, leaving bloody fingerprints on its dirty white surface. The onlookers creating a corridor between the Executioner and his quarry fell back to new perimeters when Bolan lifted the stainless-steel Magnum to arm's length.

"Put your hands on top of your head," Bolan ordered in an icy voice.

The assassin froze, arms outstretched from his body. Then he started to turn.

"You're not going to shoot him down like a goddamn dog, mister," a girl snarled as she stepped between Bolan and the assassin. Clad in patched blue jeans and wearing a jacket of the same material with the name of a street gang stitched across the back, the girl looked twentyish but Bolan doubted she had seen sixteen yet.

The look in the assassin's eyes was feral. His good hand clawed for something at his belt. Bolan lunged, snaring one of the girl's wrists in his hand and pulling her away as he squeezed the .44's trigger. Then the world exploded in a sudden rush of heat, sweeping Bolan's senses away.

3

Bringing the sand-stained BMW to a halt, the big blond-haired man surveyed the crowd that was starting to fill the Khan al-Khalili bazaar. He knew the narrow and winding streets of the area wouldn't allow the car to pass through easily, even if those streets were empty of all the pedestrians now moving about freely. He saw an occasional motorbike thread cautiously through the groups of families and friends taking in the noisy sights the bazaar had to offer.

For a moment the man let his mind drift, recalling the first time old Kettwig had taken him into the trading place. With his father's permission, of course. He'd been eight then, and had clung to Kettwig's hand the whole time. Surprisingly his father's valet had allowed the hand-holding and had said nothing. Even after that one day, it had been hard for Ris to see the valet as the grim soldier he had been while his father was alive. Even harder now that he was grown, straight and tall, while old Kettwig had bent and shriveled with age.

Reluctantly he shook away the memories. He had business there, he reminded himself, and tried to pretend that it was *only* business and that he didn't feel the loss Helene's escape had filled him with.

Weakness, he chided himself. In his mind, though, it was his father's clipped voice that reproved him and not his own.

He switched off the air-conditioning and let the engine idle for a moment, replacing the drain the unit had exacted from the battery. While he waited, he rolled his window down and let the sounds of the bazaar flood the interior of the vehicle.

Ris removed a SIG-Sauer P-226 from the glove compartment and clipped it to the back of his belt, under the jacket he wore. He tested it, satisfied it would pull free easily when he found the man he was looking for. Then he raised the window again and thumbed the electronic door lock as he got out.

Glancing around, he spotted a teenager lounging against a leather shop, watching the BMW with glittering black eyes.

"Boy," Ris called in Arabic, the syllables rolling easily from his tongue.

"Yes?"

The big man motioned the youth over, then gave him an easy smile and reached into his inside jacket pocket. "Would you like to make some money this morning?"

"Of course, but how may I serve you?" The youth's eyes kept darting to the BMW, and curiosity about the plush secrets it held inside showed on his face.

"I have something to do in the bazaar," the big man said as an image of golden-haired Helene filled his mind, "and I need someone to watch my car."

The youth cupped his chin in his hand and looked at the sand-covered pavement between his bare feet. "That is a very important job, maybe even a very dangerous one. This car is worth much money and the bazaar is filled with dangerous men."

Ris let a mirthless grin cover his face as he thumbed the crisp Egyptian pound notes in his hand. He recognized the beginning of the haggling process and fell into it automatically. He had grown up around Cairo and had done a lot of the buying for the movement himself since his father died.

He put the money away and nodded. "Perhaps you are right," he told the youth. "Maybe I should find someone older and stronger. Someone more experienced." He started to turn away.

"Wait." The boy smiled sheepishly. "Youth and speed are very good defenses, too, and my father's shop is only across the street. In effect, when you hire me, you are hiring my father as well."

"How much would you say your protection is worth?"

The youth held out a handful of fingers. "Five pounds."

The big man popped a crisp bill between his hands. "One pound."

"This is a very expensive car. Three pounds."

"I won't be gone that long. Two pounds." The big man took another bill from his pocket.

"Done," the youth said as he extended his hand.

"Done," the man agreed as he put his two pound notes away. "And you'll be paid when I return." Haggling wasn't the only art a man had to learn in Cairo, but it should always be one of the first. And the service should never be paid for until it had been provided. Otherwise the provider could insist many "unforeseen" complications had arisen that cost more.

The youth gave him a pained expression but nodded curtly. "What's your name?"

"Ris."

The youth bowed his head. "I will remain with your car, Ris, awaiting your return."

Nodding, Ris stepped into the flow of the human traffic winding through the gritty streets. For a moment claustrophobia played with the outer edges of his sanity. He had grown up in the desert, on sand hills under unfettered blue skies. Even the underground headquarters, carved from the hardened rock around the Nile hadn't seemed to press on him the same way. One step at a time, he told himself as he moved through the crowd.

A flash of long gold hair attracted his attention to a woman standing before a shop filled with alabaster carvings.

Helene. The name ripped through him like a hawk's bill.

For a moment Ris stood frozen as people moved around him. His heartbeat increased as feelings of anger, betrayal and loss soared through him, inseparable, painful.

Helene.

His weakness.

Then he saw that the woman wasn't Helene when she continued haggling with the merchant over a small, inlaid chessboard. He forced the breath from his lungs and moved on. The woman couldn't have been Helene, he thought angrily. The long blond tresses he had loved so much had been left on the floor of her room, victims of her rage.

The weight of the 9 mm pistol felt good to him as he took another left, working his way to his destination. Early this morning one of his agents had brought him information of the man he sought. Ris had left the complex without waking Kettwig, knowing the old man would advise against his seeking out Helene at this time, saying everything he did now would be crucial to the movement. There would never be a better time, Kettwig had told him only yesterday.

But the old man could only advise. Ris was still the leader, still the man who would carry them all into their vision of the world. He still made his own decisions. He just wished he could get his father out of his mind. Even now, if he closed his eyes for just a moment, he could recall every detail of his father's black uniform and the red band against his right arm, could see the stern look in his father's eyes as the man forced him through some new phase of his training. More than anything else, he could remember his father's bitterness, an almost palpable presence, that he wouldn't be the one to usher in the new world he'd worked so hard to help create.

The café loomed before Ris. Would the man he searched for know him? Ris wondered as he surveyed the front of the building. His agent had provided a photograph, taken with a small Kodak that developed instantly. Ris had given the agent bonus leave from his duty because taking any picture in Cairo without being noticed was almost an incredible feat. Would Helene still be with the man? With conscious effort, he kept his hand from the SIG-Sauer and walked toward the doors.

What if the man was no longer there? Suppose he had checked out of his room over the café and vanished with Helene? The sense of loss created a frenzy within Ris, giving rise to a sour taste at the back of his throat. He swallowed hard and stepped into the café.

The sluggish morning air was stirred about by the four ceiling fans in the corners of the small room. Their whirring noise helped block some of the bazaar conversations and haggling, lending the establishment some privacy.

Ris walked to the scarred wooden counter, scanning the morning's clientele, looking for Helene and the man. None of the eight men in the café was the one he was looking for. Two were white, and Ris watched these men with interest. Maybe they were friends of the man he was after.

The proprietor, an old man wearing a frayed turban and a stained djellaba, watched him with hooded eyes as his hands stayed busy toweling glasses dry. Leaning on the counter, Ris placed the photograph of the man Helene had been seen with between two wet spots. The proprietor feigned disinterest. Ris produced a five-pound note and placed it on top of the photo.

The proprietor finished the glass he was working on and tossed his towel across a bony shoulder as he bent for a closer look. Without replying, the man leaned back, took out an evil-smelling Egyptian cigarette, then patted his pockets in search of a light.

Ris took the diamond-studded lighter he carried from his jacket pocket and thumbed a yellow flame into wavering life. An involuntary flicker of the proprietor's eyelids signaled his sudden interest.

"Who are you?" the man asked in English.

"A man," Ris replied in Arabic. He was counting on the two men seated behind him not to speak the language in case they were with the man he was looking for. He kept watch on them by glancing over the proprietor's shoulder at the time-stained mirror behind the counter. "A man willing to pay for whatever knowledge you have of this man."

The proprietor touched the edges of the photograph without lifting it from the counter as if he were stroking a talisman. "How much would such knowledge be worth?"

"We can discuss it."

The proprietor nodded, turning his gaze back to the photograph. "I have seen this man."

"I know." Ris let the words carry an unspoken threat the man wouldn't miss.

"Would a hundred pounds be too much to ask for this information?"

"Fifty."

"Seventy-five."

"Agreed." Ris could tell by the look of displeasure on the man's face that the proprietor knew he could have easily gotten the initial asking price and that the man was trying to think of a way to renegotiate.

An objection died on the proprietor's lips when Ris leaned forward. The man rubbed his fingers and thumb together.

"Later," Ris promised, "after we talk."

Reaching below the counter, the man placed a glass before Ris and poured a shot of arrack.

Ris ignored the rumlike liquor, knowing the fiery concoction would knot up his stomach in his present emotional state.

"You are alone?"

Ris nodded.

"The man you want has companions."

"Here?"

"Yes."

"The man is still here?"

"Yes."

Ris tried hard to control his exultation. So close to Helene. So close. "The white men?" He moved his thumb in front of him so that the men at the table behind him wouldn't see the gesture.

"They," the proprietor said, "as well as the South African."

Ris tapped the picture. "Who is he?"

"They call him Callahan. He is the leader in their arms-dealing organization."

"They're small-time," Ris said, indicating their diminutive stature with his forefinger and thumb. Otherwise he would know of them.

The proprietor took the statement as a question and answered it with a nod. "Small-time as well as new. They parade their money around but drive very hard bargains in the bazaar. They lack a certain class."

"But their money is good. That's why you allow them to stay here."

The proprietor shrugged.

Ris noticed one of the men get up and approach the counter. "What room is Callahan in?"

"Three. At the top of the stairs."

Folding the pound notes, Ris slid them toward the proprietor and watched them disappear under the man's sleeve. He was sure the man behind him never saw the transaction. Pushing away from the counter, he looked at the narrow wooden stairs that led to the second floor. There were only four rooms across the back of the café, each opening out onto the runway overlooking the table area.

Ris moved up the stairs, feeling the eyes of the men on him. There would be little time once his intentions were divined. But he couldn't make himself turn away. Behind the bleak deadness of the wooden door, Helene could be waiting.

Why had she involved herself with someone like Callahan? The man looked inefficient and unkempt, from his long brown hair and cheap gold necklace to the stained camouflage jacket he wore in the photograph. Helene would never be interested in a man like that, would she?

He pushed the questions to another part of his mind, bringing the trained predator forward, the beast that his father had created during what had seemed like endless hours of grueling physical punishment.

He moved without hesitation, drawing the SIG-Sauer when he reached the top of the stairs, keeping it out of sight until he raised a big foot and sent it crashing through the door of room 3.

The lock splintered through the wood. A girl's startled yelp came to his ears, sending his adrenaline soaring.

Gripping the pistol in both hands, he swung into the room. For a moment the sight of the naked woman scrambling across the bed drew his attention. He drank in the sight of her, from the sculptured calves, the tanned thighs, the whiteness of her rounded buttocks, the impudent upthrust of her small breasts. Helene? Then he saw the face, framed by long brunette hair. Helene was blond.

He placed two shots just under the girl's left breast so that he wouldn't have to worry about her movements during the coming conflict, watching in satisfaction as her blood sprayed over the dingy yellow wallpaper behind her.

Then he aimed at Callahan as the arms runner fumbled for a mini-Uzi cached between the mattresses of the bed. Moving the open sights from the chin covered by a three-day growth of beard, Ris dispassionately shot the man through the right shoulder.

Callahan gave a pained grunt and spun away from the machine pistol, falling across the corpse of the girl.

Ris moved across the room and scooped up the weapon, settling it comfortably in his left hand.

"Goddamn son of a bitch," Callahan screamed as he launched himself from the bed. He had his arms spread wide, and blood spurted from the shoulder wound.

Shifting his weight, Ris dealt the arms dealer a round-house kick that propelled the man backward into the wall. He fitted himself into the meager shelter offered by the door and levered the mini-Uzi into target acquisition.

The machine pistol stuttered into life as Callahan's two companions came charging up the stairs to aid their comrade. The clip ran dry as Ris moved it in a flesh-shredding figure eight that blew both men over the second-floor railing.

Ris had to step forward to find the South African. He tossed the mini-Uzi over the broken railing and raised the SIG-Sauer. Sighting carefully, moving the open sights after the fleeing man, he squeezed softly when he had the man's neck centered. The bullet drove the man's spine into the back of his throat and pitched him facefirst onto the floor.

There was no sign of the proprietor.

Ris returned to the room just as Callahan was throwing a leg over the open window. He triggered another round, which crashed through the man's right knee.

Callahan toppled to the floor, writhing in agony. Harsh screams, filled with pain and anger, ripped from his lips. "You're dead, you bastard. You're dead."

Placing the heated barrel of the SIG-Sauer to Callahan's forehead, Ris forced the man's head to the floor.

Callahan closed his eyes, whimpering.

Ris let the man wait.

Then, after the sobbing had subsided somewhat and because he knew it would only be a matter of minutes before the Tourist Police arrived from the bazaar, he asked in a soft voice, "Where's the girl?"

"I don't know what you're talking about, man," Callahan screamed. "You killed the girl. Christ."

"Where's the girl?" Ris repeated. "The blonde?"

"I don't know what you're talking about."

Moving the pistol, Ris triggered a round that dug splinters from the wooden floor beside the man's left ear. Callahan squirmed away from the floor, screaming in renewed agony.

"The girl," Ris demanded. Painful images of Callahan and Helene making love tumbled through his mind. "Where's Helene?"

"Christ, I don't know, man. Honest I don't. She picked me up at this café two days ago. She said she needed me and talked me into letting her stay the night. When I woke up, she was gone, and so was my money belt. I've been looking for her, too, but it's like she dropped off the edge of the world."

For the first time since Helene had escaped two days ago, Ris felt a cold chill penetrate his gut. Was she dead, then? No. He pushed the thought away. No, if she was dead, he would have felt it. She was out there somewhere. Still running.

He returned his attention to Callahan. "Did you enjoy making love to her, American?"

Blood seeped through Callahan's fingers from his shoulder wound. "I didn't touch her. She wouldn't let me. She damn near scratched my eyes out when I got close to her." He indicated days-old scratches on his forehead with a bloody finger.

"Good," Ris said, then emptied his pistol's clip methodically into Callahan's face.

4

Leo Turrin dropped the AK-47 and ran, following the line of police cars to the front of the video arcade. Kirby Howell limped after him. The whirling cherry glare of the patrol cars' flashing lights ignited the scene for Turrin, splashing haphazardly over the shocked and angry faces of the jeans-clad clientele staring at the broken windows of the building. Smoke eddied gently from the windows, pulled along by the hot, dry wind.

The Fed cut across the street into oncoming traffic. Brakes locked and screeched as drivers swerved to miss him. Once he had to place his hands on the hood of an older Chevy to keep from falling under its wheels. Then he was across.

Mack couldn't be dead, Turrin told himself. But the smashed and broken windows told another story. Flames still licked at the tiled ceiling overhead, and the smoke inside was too thick to allow his vision to penetrate much more than a yard or two at best. Not Mack. The guy was supposed to be indestructible. How many times had he seen the big guy square off against impossible odds only to walk away the winner? Images chased themselves through his mind, from the time in Pittsfield when the Executioner was putting the finishing touches on Sergio Frenchi's Mob to the events in the office building down the street. Always Bolan had escaped to fight another day. A walking nightmare in executioner black.

A beefy policeman with a florid face and iron-gray hair stepped in front of Turrin and grabbed him by the shoulder. "Hold on now, mister," the cop said as Turrin struggled free. "You just stand back out of the way."

Turrin flashed his Justice credentials. He looked past the cop, trying to see some sign of Bolan. "I've got a friend in there, damn it."

The cop drew back with an apologetic look.

The Fed brushed by the man, pulling a handkerchief from his shirt pocket and clamping it over his nose and mouth as he entered the building. He bent low, searching through the layers of smoke with tearing eyes. What the hell had happened? He scanned the wreckage of the video machines. An explosion, sure, but where had it come from?

Judging from the pockmarked holes in the walls where bits of flame still clung tenaciously, Turrin assumed the bomb had been incendiary in nature.

His left foot shot out from under him, and he almost went down, his left hand taking the weight of the fall. The greasy texture of blood covered his fingers, and he dragged his hand across his pant leg without looking.

A dark shadow swirled in the smoke before him, and he fell back into the cover of a nearby video machine, arm extended with the Bodyguard at the end of it.

"Easy, Leo," said a familiar voice.

"Mack?"

"Yeah."

"You okay?"

"I think so."

"What happened?"

"I caught the guy I was after," Bolan explained as he moved forward.

Leo saw the big warrior weave uncertainly for a moment, then shake his head as if to clear it. It was hard to separate Bolan's smudged features from the clouded air.

"He blew himself up when he saw there was no way out. A girl stepped between us, trying to keep me away from the guy. She took the brunt of the explosion. I guess I was out for a few minutes."

Moving forward, Turrin took one of Bolan's arms across his shoulders, helping support the bigger man as they weaved through the burned out husks of the game machines. At first Bolan tried to resist the help, stubbornly trying to make it on his own. Turrin knew it was more a survival mechanism than a macho hang-up. Bolan wasn't used to operating in an environment where helping hands were extended without a price or without treachery in mind.

"Lean on me, Mack. It's a wonder you're on your feet at all." Then he was guiding them through the door, holstering the .38 to produce the Justice credentials for the waiting cops, bitching loudly when one of the uniforms didn't clear the area fast enough. He demanded a car and got one, then helped the warrior into the back seat. Turrin sat beside him after rolling the windows down, feeling the burning ache deep in his lungs and knowing Bolan's had to be in worse shape.

He saw the warrior pry his eyes open to look at him, saw the wary hunter glinting in the volcanic blue. He knew Bolan was out on his feet but refused to stay under until he reached some safe harbor.

"Chill out, Sarge," Turrin encouraged quietly. "I got this watch." He laid the .38 across his thighs meaningfully.

Bolan nodded and closed his eyes.

HAL BROGNOLA STOOD just inside the darkened office, feeling the stress and the hours of tiredness wash over him. There was a sense of comfort in the room, though, because Bolan would be sitting behind the desk in the morning poring over the security plans for the Russians' visit. And even though the man had yet to set foot in the room, Brognola had no trouble imagining him sitting in the swivel chair.

Taking a cigar from an inside jacket pocket, Brognola peeled off the wrapper and stuck the cigar into a corner of his mouth, experiencing an almost spiritual moment of relief from the action. He checked his watch again. Good. It was still another thirty minutes until the press conference took place downstairs. Time enough for him to get his head together before going full-tilt against the reporters who would be waiting for the no-news that would be the only thing they would be given. So far no one had tipped to anything definite about a threat against Gorbachev's life. Which, considering how many of the alphabet agencies in the capital knew, was pretty goddamn amazing.

Even though there was a certain satisfaction in the President's decision to coordinate activities with and through the Justice Department, Brognola was shouldering a lot of the weight of responsibility. In light of the black eye Justice received during the previous President's tenure, the big Fed was glad for the opportunity to garner a little praise while the visit was in the limelight, start building a more positive image for the Department.

As long as nothing went wrong.

A shadow drifted across the light spilling into Brognola's office, letting him know he wasn't alone anymore. He shifted the unlit cigar and turned slowly.

The expression on Greg Bowen's face was more of a smirk than a smile, and it irritated Brognola that the younger man had slipped up on him undetected.

Bowen was as tall as Brognola, but thinner, possessing the broad chest of a weight lifter and tapering down to a narrow waist. As a section chief for the CIA on this operation, Bowen held an almost equal rank with the head Fed, even though he hadn't seen thirty yet. Brognola wasn't sure which bothered him most in their two-week-old relationship: the way Bowen looked in the expensive clothes he wore, or the insouciant grin that habitually played with the man's lips.

"Penny for your thoughts, Hal," Bowen said as Brognola stepped from the office and locked the door behind him.

"You'd be overspending," Brognola replied, "even in these inflationary times."

Bowen folded his arms across his chest and leaned against the wall by the office door.

Brognola looked for a telltale crease in the jacket that would reveal the agent's shoulder holster, thinking he might sink a barb about the guy finding a new tailor. But there wasn't one.

The grin stayed on Bowen's face. "I'm told this Belasko guy is going to be operating directly with your group on this."

Brognola nodded warily, wondering where the conversation was heading. Kurtzman had kept him up on all the investigative attempts the different agencies had made to penetrate the wall of biographies and manufactured history that had been grafted onto Bolan's cover. There had been dozens. The interest, expected as it had been, had still almost been enough to shake the Man's resolve to include Bolan in the security net.

"So, tell me, Hal," Bowen said, "just between you and me. What's the deal with Belasko?"

"He's here as a security consultant, at the President's request."

"Yeah, I know all that, Hal. I even know his grandmother's maiden name. On both sides of the family tree. What I don't know is why I've never heard of this guy if he's so good."

Brognola flashed the younger man an easy smile of his own. It felt good to be one up on Bowen. He'd be damned if he'd admit it to anyone, but it did feel good. "Belasko operates under a low profile." He started down the hallway toward the elevator.

Bowen fell into step beside him. "I operate under a low profile, too, but people have heard of me."

"Maybe it's because you've got a better tailor or better hairdresser."

"Maybe it's because I'm good at what I do," Bowen said. "You know many section chiefs in the Central Intelligence Agency that made section chief before they hit thirty?"

"So what are we talking about here, kid? Professional jealousy? You looking to make your bones on this one, or what?" Brognola had to give the younger man credit, though, because Bowen showed no visible reaction to his taunt.

"You got the professional part right, Hal. That's what keeps bugging me about your guy, Belasko. I've been planning this little caper for a couple of months. I knew about you at that time. I knew about the FBI people who were going to be involved. I dug up profiles on the NSA heads who were slated to handle this visit. I had a handle on every one of them at least a month ago. But not one word trickled into these sensitive little ears of mine about a Michael Belasko until the day before yesterday.''

Brognola pushed the button for the elevator and looked at Bowen. ''That's when I got the call through to him.''

''How long had you been indecisive about calling him in to ramrod this for you?''

''So now we're going to talk about my professionalism?'' Brognola let a little hardness creep into his voice. The kid was sharp and determined, but by pursuing his present line of questioning he could very well upset one of the best defenses the Russians could have.

''Indecisiveness is a bad sign, Hal. If you were going to call Belasko in, I don't understand why you didn't do it earlier. Seems to me, a guy with the kind of reputation Mr. Belasko enjoys wouldn't be able to drop everything he was doing and come running at a moment's notice.''

''We got lucky,'' Brognola replied, and meant it. It had taken Bolan almost twenty-four hours to return his call.

''Two days ago,'' Bowen went on, ''I start hearing Mike Belasko's name. Two days ago I start hearing little tidbits about a suspected assassination attempt. Now tell me, is that a coincidence or what?''

Placing a big hand on the open elevator doors, Brognola leaned forward, invading the younger man's space, breathing hard on the CIA man's cheek. ''Don't ever let me get the idea you're accusing me or my department of one goddamn thing,'' he said in a low voice, ''or I'll kick your skinny ass.''

Bowen's hazel eyes frosted over and his smile tightened. ''You're giving away a lot of years, Granddad.''

"And all of them well spent in learning how to kick the ass of every young pup who annoyed me."

Glancing at the diamond-studded Rolex at the end of his arm, Bowen said, "We better get a move on if we're going to make the press conference. We can feel each other's muscles on the way down."

Brognola stepped inside the cage and made room for Bowen. He stabbed the floor number.

"Do you just dislike me?" the younger man asked.

"Right now I dislike everyone."

Bowen grinned and shoved his hands into his pockets. "Everyone except Belasko, you mean."

Brognola didn't bother to reply.

The elevator doors hissed open. A crowd of newspeople filled the hallway leading to the conference room. Heads started turning as Brognola stepped out with Bowen in tow. A warning itch flared up between his shoulder blades when most of the crowd rushed at him and minicams turned in his direction, flickering into sudden life.

Before he had taken three steps, Brognola walked into a barrage of microphones, hearing the different identifying preamble each reporter made. Questions were fired at him from point-blank range with machine gun efficiency.

"Is Michael Belasko working with the Justice Department to protect the Soviet representatives?"

"Are you Harold Brognola?"

"Is Belasko operating under your orders?"

"What do you know of the shootings that occurred in the southeast office area?"

"Did you know reliable sources are saying Belasko killed a half-dozen men tonight?"

"Do you believe someone working for the Justice Department should court violence in the streets of this city?"

"What are your feelings about the use of deadly force by law-enforcement personnel?"

"Have you heard whether Belasko lived through the bomb blast?"

Brognola raised his hands and motioned the crowd to silence, aware that Bowen had moved unnoticed to the outside fringe of the reporters. A curious look filled the man's handsome face, and Brognola knew even when he answered all the questions the reporters had, there would still be ones to answer for Bowen. What the hell had Striker stepped into tonight?

HELENE USED HER FINGERS to trace the shiny curvature of the necklace through the glass of the display case, wondering how it would feel against her skin. Would it be cool? Or would it draw in the desert heat until it almost reached a burning point? It would certainly be heavy. Gold always was, weighted with wealth and with the sins that were made to earn it.

But Ris wouldn't know anything of that, she told herself. To Ris, gold meant power. Nothing more.

She turned away from the dark thoughts, almost afraid that if she thought too much or too long about Ris that those thoughts would draw him to her like a vulture to a fresh kill.

The money belt she had taken from the American yesterday morning was still full. She didn't know how much money was in the compartments but hoped it would be enough to see her clear of Cairo. As soon as she figured out a way through the gauntlet Ris was sure to have waiting for her. It was certain he would have informants at airports and bus stations looking for her. The taxi drivers were out of the question, as well. The last time she had escaped, one of them had turned her in for the reward Ris had offered.

Helene was all too aware of Ris's anger, of the madness he held in check, knowing that she wasn't dead now only because Ris wanted her. Revulsion filled her as she remembered the touch of Ris's hands on her body. How many times had he forced himself on her? Sometimes he would stay away, but Helene knew he was only testing himself, trying to see if his addiction to her would pass with abstinence. But, as always, he would eventually return to her, seeking solace from whatever devils preyed on his mind. He would lose himself in her flesh. Afterward, Helene would lock herself in the small bathroom adjoining her bedroom/prison and hunker under the spray until it turned cold and Ris left. Even then she hadn't felt clean. She hadn't for months.

"Will there be anything else, mistress?"

Reluctantly Helene glanced up at the old woman behind the counter as the sounds of the bazaar flooded in on her. She shook her head and reached into her newly purchased djellaba for money. "How much?" she asked, indicating the salves and creams she had selected to protect her pale skin from the harsh desert wind and sun. She had been unprepared for the scorching heat after living in the underground complex for so long.

The old woman named a sum.

Helene sorted through her money, choosing smaller bills so that memory of her would be lessened.

"I can make you a good deal on the necklace," the old woman said.

"No, thank you," Helene said as she started to hand the bills over. The money belt she had found on Calla-

han had been an unexpected treasure. Yesterday she had
lived on the scraps from expensive motels and caught
small naps in out-of-the-way corners of the bazaar. Every
pound note in her possession when she found the means
would tip the scales in favor of her freedom when the
time came to escape.

A slender hand with expensively manicured nails
wrapped tapered fingers around Helene's wrist, holding
her arm back. Helene fought the instinctive urge to flee,
thinking the hand belonged to one of Ris's agents.

But a woman stepped forward, releasing Helene.
"Before she even discusses any deals for the necklace,"
the unknown woman said, "she would first like a decent
price for the cosmetics she is purchasing."

The old woman behind the counter made a face.

Helene, still fighting to control the anxiety raging in
her, studied the woman who had interceded on her be-
half. The woman was half a head shorter, which wasn't
surprising because Helene found herself taller than many
men, even the soldiers Ris worked out with in the gym-
nasium. The woman's long brown hair, almost the same
hue as her dark eyes, was piled on top of her head in a
style Helene hadn't seen before. Her appearance was re-
gal, proportioned generously beneath the faded black
jeans ensemble she wore. Her skin tone was shades
darker than the collar of the white silk blouse she wore
under the short-waisted jacket. American, Helene
thought, because of the woman's dress and the way she
conducted herself. Wealthy, too, judging from the glittering array of jewelry adorning the woman's neck and
hands.

"The price has already been agreed on," the Arab
woman said.

The American raised one perfectly arched eyebrow. "You have the money?"

"The price has been agreed on."

The woman turned to Helene. "Put your money away, child, and we will go somewhere else. Surely someone here will quote us a fair price."

Helene stood undecided about what to do. She had been on the move, fearing for her life, for the past two days. Maybe an argument over prices was a commonplace experience for the woman, but it could get her killed or, worse, recaptured. She didn't know if she could survive being a prisoner again, assuming Ris let her live.

"Wait," the counterwoman said.

The American turned around and the dickering began in earnest. Finally, to Helene's relief, she seemed satisfied with the price and let Helene give the Arab woman the money.

"Thank you," Helene said as they walked away from the cosmetic stand. Inside she wished the woman would go away. The woman's beauty set her apart too much, made too many men look at her. How long would it be, Helene wondered anxiously, before one of those men staring at the American woman was loyal to Ris? In the djellaba with her hair cut to a length hardly longer than a man's, Helene was sure she would go unnoticed for the most part. Her height was compensated for by the short hair, and she was convinced the sexless djellaba prompted many people to think she was a man.

"What's your name, child?" the American woman asked.

"Krista," Helene answered. It had been her mother's name. Only the knowledge of that and the small handful of pictures she had been permitted to retain were all she had of her mother.

The woman offered her hand.

Helene took it, surprised again at the strength of it.

"I'm Constance McKenna," the woman said, smiling warmly.

"It's nice to meet you," Helene replied, and wished it was true. She tried to think of a way to slip away from the woman and fade back into the crowd of the bazaar. She had to be by herself, she thought, until she could think of a way to get out of Cairo. It surprised her to learn that part of her wanted to remain with the woman and share the companionship she offered. Only occasionally had she had any contact with other women, and then only ones Ris employed to groom and dress her before one of his visits.

"Is this your first time in the bazaar?" Constance asked.

"Yes," Helene replied truthfully.

The woman's eyes flashed with dark glints as she looked around the crowded thoroughfare. "I assume you're alone?"

Helene nodded.

"A young woman like you shouldn't be in this bazaar alone. There's no telling what might happen. True, there are the Tourist Police to protect you, but they can't be everywhere at once. In fact, just this morning I heard there was some sort of massacre at one of the cafés near here. A mercenary unit between jobs, I think. The authorities believe the men were trying to muscle in on one of the local drug suppliers."

"Callahan," Helene said before she could stop herself.

Constance flashed her a brief smile devoid of any humor. "I believe that was the name of one of the men. How do you know them?"

Helene looked away. Was the meeting in the bazaar by chance or by design? Was Ris involved? Callahan's death was surely at Ris's hands. Someone had spotted her with the mercenary and told Ris. A cold fear speared down the back of her neck as she realized again how truly alone and unprotected she was. "I don't really. I had an unsavory experience with them yesterday."

The woman nodded in response, but Helene sensed she didn't really believe her.

Helene stopped abruptly. "I'm sorry to rush off like this," she said, straining not to continually look over her shoulder, "but I really have to be going."

"Can I walk you somewhere?"

Helene shook her head. "No, thank you."

The older woman's eyes narrowed. "You're in trouble, aren't you?" The woman's voice was calm and measured, and too low to be heard by the many passersby.

Helene met her gaze with trouble. Was this one of Ris's tricks, or was this woman for real? Was she passing up the opportunity to leave Cairo by not telling her everything?

In the end caution won and Helene said nothing.

A heavy sigh slipped through Constance McKenna's painted lips. "I don't know what kind of trouble you're fleeing from, child, and God knows I'm old enough to know better than to get involved, but if you find you need someone, come see me. I'm staying at the Hilton." The woman scribbled something on a small card and held it out.

Trembling inside, Helene reached for it, noting the name and room number printed in block letters. Tears of helplessness stung her eyes as she held on to the card and fled deeper into the bazaar. She wished she could have trusted the woman, could have been sure that Constance McKenna would have helped her.

5

Mack Bolan forced himself to stand under the cold water of the shower's needlelike spray until goose bumps rose on his skin. He was still sore from the explosion in the arcade four hours earlier. The chill drove the final remnants of fog from his mind, though, and restored circulation to his limbs. There was still a slight ringing in his ears, but it wasn't overly annoying at the moment.

He stepped from the shower stall and into the terry cloth warmth of the plush towel he found waiting. His mirror image stared back at him with baleful red eyes. He ignored the numerous scars crisscrossing his upper body, knowing they bespoke a violent past and foretold a violent future. He quickly finished toweling himself and dressed in jeans and a knit shirt. After checking to make sure the Desert Eagle and Beretta were fully charged, he gathered his shoulder rigging in one hand and started for the door, grabbing the new pair of joggers sitting on the edge of the sink as he walked past.

He padded barefoot across the carpet, feeling at home. Or at least as much at home as he had felt in years. Even at three o'clock in the morning there was an undercurrent of life that beat beneath the bulletproof skin of Stony Man Farm, deep in the Blue Ridge Mountains of Virginia.

He paused in the large dining room, fisting a pair of peaches from the bowl of fruit on the dark sideboard, then made his way down a short hallway to Aaron Kurtzman's world, the computer room.

World was the correct choice of word, Bolan thought again as he closed the door behind him quietly. The huge room was filled with the latest in high-tech equipment and computers. There were linkups within the walls of the room that could access information, discreetly, from a large portion of the satellites in frozen orbit above the earth, many of them under the influence and control of other countries. Other components diffused the signal and retriangulated it away from Stony Man and Kurtzman. Still more allowed the Bear's cybernetic fingers to flip through records through phone lines, securing the information in nanoseconds, then displaying or copying it for later reference.

Aaron Kurtzman sat at a half-moon-shaped console near the center of the room, his fingers idly toying with the keyboard in front of him. His lips flexed as Bolan observed him, pushing in and out the way they always did when the Bear was involved in a problem. Bolan laid his shoulder rigging and joggers on a nearby desk.

Kurtzman's head swiveled around in response to the noise, and a smile split his big face. "Hey, Mack."

"Aaron." Bolan stepped forward and took the big man's hand, almost losing his fingers in the enormous grip. If it hadn't been for the wheelchair, Kurtzman would have towered over him. Bolan had often thought Kurtzman must have had shoulders that made his mother cry every time she bought his clothes. Even in his diminished stature, Kurtzman was one hell of a big man.

"Coffee's on," Kurtzman said as he rolled back from the console.

Bolan nodded and padded over to the coffee maker set up against the wall. The liquid in the glass pot looked dark and evil, and he wondered if his stomach was ready for anything as vile as the concoction Kurtzman habitually brewed.

"You'll find a real cup under the cabinet behind the napkins," Kurtzman told him. "I can't get the housekeeping staff to understand that a man has the right to drink out of a man's cup."

Bolan knelt for a moment and reached into the cabinet past the Styrofoam cups and packages of napkins, finding two more broad-based ceramic mugs. He took one and lifted the pot from the coffee machine on his way back to Kurtzman. He filled the big man's cup and poured the dregs into his own. "You ever think about making a fresh pot?" he asked as he started a new brewing cycle. "That could be part of the problem with the Styrofoam cups."

Kurtzman waved the thought away. "Hell, I change it every three days whether it needs it or not."

Bolan chuckled. He took a seat on Kurtzman's console, cupping the coffee mug in both hands to combat the chill of the room, his bare feet dangling inches above the floor. "Where's Leo?"

"I put him up in one of the other bedrooms. The man was out on his feet."

"I know. Did he call Angelina?"

"Yeah. They talked for a little while. Long enough for him to tell her he was still alive and not to expect him home right away."

"How's he holding up?"

"You know Leo. He's spent too many years holding his feelings in to just open up and say what's on his mind."

Kurtzman pushed a button on the console, and the room's lights dimmed. A panel on the far wall slid back to reveal a forty-eight-inch screen. "I didn't find any dirt on that cop of yours." He stabbed at another button, and a black-and-white still of the policeman's face filled the screen. The cop looked younger in the photograph, eager to please.

"His name's Dwight Hooker," Kurtzman said in a monotone. "He's been a D.C. cop for eight years, has a clean record except for a minor traffic accident in a squad car about six years ago. According to his files, he's never used his gun the entire time he's been on the force, never been cited for using excessive force. He lives in Fairfax and works a part-time job at Spraggue Industries as a security guard."

The screen ran through an assembly of paperwork, personal biographies, merit evaluations, shooting range scores, interspersed with a couple of more pictures of Hooker that must have been shot for local newspapers. Bolan didn't try to read the captions, searching, instead, for a fix on the man.

"What makes you so sure this guy pinned the bug on your car?" Kurtzman asked.

"I called you to put the paperwork through on the car when I rolled it out of the garage at Justice," Bolan said. "Nobody knew which car I was going to be driving until I was on the road."

"Someone could have bugged all the unassigned cars in the garage," Kurtzman suggested.

Bolan sipped his coffee, watching as the initial picture of Officer Hooker slid back into frame and stopped. "Yeah, but I checked the car before I took it. Hooker is the only person who touched it besides me."

"Could be some kind of interdepartmental play, somebody in the FBI or Secret Service trying to figure you out. As far as the other security teams are concerned, you're the only wild card in the game, the only guy who's not really family."

"Maybe," Bolan conceded, "but at this stage of the play, we can't afford to take chances."

Kurtzman grunted an affirmative. "Hal called while you were in the shower and said he'd call back."

"How did he sound?"

"As gruff as ever," Kurtzman answered with a grin.

Bolan drained his cup and returned for the pot. "What have you got on the Witness Protection murders?"

Kurtzman punched commands into the keyboard as he answered. "I broke into the AP and UPI hookups first after Leo gave me the names he had, and cross-referenced the microfiche for any mention of the Witness Protection Program people. Apparently no one has made the connection between the murders, or the program heads are sitting on this one." The screen on the wall darkened again, then flickered back into quick life. News stories paraded across the large screen, bringing an alternate reality into the cloistered crispness of the Bear's world.

"Whole families killed to the last member," Kurtzman said. "Leo was right about that."

"Any idea who's behind it?"

"No." Kurtzman cleared the screen and the keys clicked under his fingertips as he fed in new commands. He faded from view as documentation fell into place over the glaring rectangle of light at the other end of the room. "I retrieved files from the local cops, district attorneys' offices, federal reports, everybody who was connected with this in any way, shape, or form. Everybody seems to agree that these were professional hits because of the way and extent to which they were carried out.''

"They're definitely not underfinanced, either," Bolan said, thinking of the helicopter attempt earlier.

"No. According to the handful of witnesses who have been available at the scenes, the men doing the killing use automatic weapons and seem to be part of some paramilitary unit because of the way they act in tandem with each other."

"That fits with what went down tonight."

The wall slid back in place over the screen and the lights came on. Bolan narrowed his eyes and watched Kurtzman blink his vision back to normal.

"Leo mentioned you got your guy to safety tonight," Kurtzman said.

Bolan sipped the coffee as the information the big man had gathered churned through his mind. "Yeah, but it definitely seemed touch-and-go there for a while."

"What does it sound like to you, Mack? I can see the wheels spinning around inside your head from here."

"I'm not sure yet, but it feels wrong. The operation seems too big, too expensive to justify. How many of those witnesses hit were still involved in court cases where their testimony was crucial?"

Kurtzman faced a small monitor in front of him and played a solo on the keyboard. "Only two," he answered as he turned back to face Bolan.

"So the other hits were scheduled as revenge?"

"It's the only possibility you have left," Kurtzman said. "Assuming the same team is doing the assassinations."

Bolan ticked off points. "Every news story you dredged up mentioned the use of automatic weapons, the fact that the families were killed to the last person, even if some of those members were elsewhere at the time of the initial attack, and that they were all supposedly under the protection of the Witness Protection Program. I think we're justified in assuming they were murdered by the same people." He slid off the table and started pacing. He pushed sleep away, wishing the caffeine in the coffee would start kicking in. "My only problem lies in how much the tab would be for an operation this size."

"You're dealing with Mafia bucks, Sarge," Kurtzman pointed out. "And you're dealing with guys who deal revenge on the installment plan, as if it's a currency. You know that."

"Yeah, I know that, but I also know that whoever is heading up this strike force is operating outside the Family."

"How do you figure that?"

"Not all of those people had testified, or were testifying against, the same Family, Aaron. If this was a Family operation, the strike force would take care of Family business and it would end there. They wouldn't move across Family lines to hire out for other Families."

Kurtzman returned to the keyboard. After a moment he said, "Okay, you've got cases spread across the continental United States. Eight names popped up in the Witness Protection people's reports, from New York to Florida and all the way out to California. But what makes you sure they wouldn't help each other out?"

"You've got to know an enemy to fight him, Aaron," Bolan said. "I fought the Mafia for years. I know what kind of offspring they breed. This is a high-profile operation, not the kind of thing most Families would go in for. No, somewhere out there we've got a guy who's auctioning off the services of his own private army. But how he can finance the type of weaponry I've seen on what the Families would be willing to pay is beyond me."

Kurtzman didn't respond and sat waiting with his fingers laced across his stomach.

"The explosion in the game room is something else I can't explain," Bolan said. "The guy I had cornered set those charges off only after he decided he couldn't escape. It wasn't as much an attempt to kill me as to avoid capture. Money can't buy that kind of loyalty. There's more to this than a simple revenge-for-hire operation. What did you get on the men I put down at the office building?"

"Nothing," Kurtzman replied flatly. "Somebody mopped up after the hit. I snared a line on the Tach channel the local guys were using only a little while ago. The SWAT teams went in expecting to find wounded in the halls and recovered only corpses."

"They haven't been able to make any of the bodies?"

"No, and they're not going to be able to, either. From the reports I pulled, the officer in charge of the investigation thinks somebody used a flamethrower on the bodies. There's still an outside chance on the fingerprints, though, but the reports weren't too hopeful."

Bolan turned away, his combat senses flaring wildly. There was no question in his mind that something more than what met the eye was going down. But what? The operation he had witnessed had been too thorough, too military, to be just a slipshod arrangement. But was the end result just murder for hire? "I'm going to need some things, Aaron."

"Name it."

"I want a pilot and a plane for starters," Bolan said as he walked across the room and slipped into the shoulder rigging, "with a helicopter waiting at the other end. And I'll need a car. Something sporty and expensive."

"Where to?" Kurtzman was one with the keyboard now. Green characters spread themselves across the monitor with astonishing speed.

"New York," Bolan answered as he pulled on the joggers.

"Any place in particular?"

"Yeah. Get me a current address on Patrizio Madrano."

Kurtzman slid on a telephone headset and got a connection. After a moment he turned away. "Patterson will meet you on the field outside as soon as you can get there. Is there anything else?"

"A card."

"What kind of card?"

"A calling card for Madrano," the Executioner said. "Make it an ace of spades."

FRITZ KETTWIG CLUMPED heavily down the halls of the underground complex, favoring his crippled knee more than usual.

Guards assigned to different nerve centers of the complex stood in front of their respective posts like carved images. Of the three men he could see, he was sure not one of them would flinch if he was to strike them with the aluminum cane he leaned on. But let someone try to compromise their security, and they would react like the vicious animals they were trained to be.

Kettwig wanted nothing more than to return to his quarters and soak the knee in Epsom salts. Maybe once he was in the whirlpool and halfway through a good bottle of schnapps, maybe then the blinding pain that plagued him would be brought to rest.

But he couldn't.

Not now.

There was still the issue of Helene's latest escape and Ris's inevitable pursuit to resolve. And the countdown in Washington, D.C., continued unchecked. If the meeting was to go off as expected, many plans that Kettwig had helped formulate over the past four decades could possibly become unraveled, with no chance for any kind of salvation.

He could feel the guards' eyes on him as he passed, but was unable to catch them looking directly at him. Their drill officers had turned out good men, the only kind of men that would fit into the new order of the world Kettwig had helped envision.

Silently he damned the pain that dug at him with dulled incisors, and damned Ris and his father, as well. Both men were charismatic, born to lead, Kettwig reflected as he pushed himself along in quiet agony, but it was men like him who assured their successes. God, it felt like the damn leg was going to fall off for sure this time.

And it didn't help that like father, like son, the insanity that plagued the elder man was surely echoed in Ris. Perhaps if Ris had been raised under his hand alone, perhaps then the problem with Helene would never have arisen. Kettwig could have guided him in different ways, expanded his sense of sexuality until Ris controlled it, had an appetite for it, instead of being devoured by it.

But that was an old argument, Kettwig told himself bitterly, and now wasn't the time to be raising old arguments.

He walked through the glassed-in receiving room where the duty corporal sat monitoring the hallways on four different television screens, briefly acknowledging the snappy salute the lower-ranked man gave him.

The lights weren't on in Ris's office, but that wasn't unusual. The younger man rarely spent any time there. He was definitely his father's child, more content in the training rooms working on hand-to-hand combat techniques, or on the underground target ranges than helming the business end of their endeavor.

Kettwig unlocked his office door. The stark severity of it made him feel more at peace, more in control of the events that were starting to spill around him like haphazardly stacked dominoes. Gratefully he sank into the plush chair behind the desk and used both hands to prop up his leg. The pain immediately lessened but didn't go away. But then it never did.

Kettwig thumbed the intercom button and buzzed the duty corporal.

"Sir?"

"Has there been any word?"

"No, sir."

"What about our away teams?"

"Nothing since the first transmission, sir."

"I want a report of that first transmission on my desk in fifteen minutes."

"Yes, sir."

Kettwig broke the connection. Damn it. A full third of the first away team had been killed or wounded in the last assault, and no one was sure if their anonymity had been broken or not. Helene was loose and free to tell everything she knew of the complex. And Ris was lost in pursuit of her instead of here. He thumbed the intercom button again.

"Sir?"

"Get Eric Konig into my office immediately."

"Yes, sir."

Reaching into a bottom drawer, Kettwig recovered a bottle of his favorite schnapps and a glass. He had stopped taking the pain pills two days ago when the date of the assassination neared, wanting to keep a clear head. But the liquor was something he could handle, a friend with whom he was accustomed to sharing dark, pain-racked nights. He drank half the glass in one swallow, feeling the liquid burn its way down to his stomach.

Swiveling his head, he focused on the faded black-and-white picture framed under a too-large glass on the wall to his left. It was too far away for him to make out the details—his eyesight had deteriorated over the years—but he knew it on the canvas of his mind. There were three men in the picture—himself, Ris's father and Field Marshal Erwin Rommel. It had been taken the day a British rifle bullet shattered his knee beyond repair. Perhaps he would have died that day if events had progressed otherwise. If it hadn't been for Ris's father, whose plans Kettwig had been included in even then.

Someone knocked lightly on the door.

"Enter," Kettwig ordered.

Konig stepped into the office, closing the door behind him. He stood tall and straight before the desk, his eyes aimed at some point on the wall above Kettwig's head.

Kettwig felt pride swell in him when he surveyed the soldier. The German blood never truly thinned. Oh, you could taint it from time to time, but it ran in the veins of excellent soldiers just as surely as oil kept engines moving smoothly. He had been a soldier just as Konig was now, dressed in the same black colors with only minor uniform alterations. The swastika was no longer worn around the upper arm, having been shifted to a shoulder patch instead. He enjoyed seeing the soldiers in full dress, and they always came that way when they were summoned to his office. It took him back years, before the crippling bullet and before age had taken his teeth, hair and strength.

"You summoned me, sir?"

Kettwig often found himself wishing for a swagger stick at times like these, but had never managed a flair for one. "Yes, Captain. I have a duty I want you to perform. One that I want you to tell no one about."

Konig said nothing.

"Do I make myself clear, Captain?"

"Of course, General."

"You are, I'm sure, aware of Helene's recent escape?"

"Yes, sir."

"Just as you are aware the meeting in America is scheduled for tomorrow?"

"Yes, sir."

"Ris is searching for Helene. The reports I have say she's been seen in the bazaar. You and I are both aware how important Ris's involvement with the plan is, of how important it is that he keeps his mind on our objective. He'll be a driving force for our order once everything has been put into play between Russia and the United States. After all, he has his father's gift for attracting people when he's placed in front of a crowd. Our experts are predicting a large turnover in the United States once our initial mission is successfully completed, considering America's own resources of the Aryan Guard and the Ku Klux Klan who will flock to us once the battle is joined. Ris will expedite these matters. But he must have a clear mind during this time."

"Yes, sir."

Kettwig could hear the excitement in the captain's reply, felt it resonate in his old, tired bones with a new energy he had almost forgotten. He was embarking on dangerous ground here. Many of the military men at the complex had sworn allegiance to Ris because he spent a lot of time with them, improving his skills and theirs, and because the whole operation had been planned around him. His father had known the importance of having one leader, and Ris was it. Captain Konig was a different sort, though. Kettwig had personally groomed the man through his last three promotions. "Helene is a problem Ris shouldn't have to deal with."

The captain looked at him for the first time. "I agree wholeheartedly, sir."

Kettwig felt a smile stretch his lower face. "I want you to find the woman before Ris does, Captain, and put her someplace he can never find her again. The desert has a delightful way of picking up after itself."

The captain's cold eyes glittered darkly.

"That's all, Captain."

"Thank you, sir." Konig saluted and let himself out.

Kettwig settled back in the chair and filled his empty glass. His eyes found the photograph again. There was a small pang of guilt over ordering the girl's death, but he crushed it before it had a chance to develop. Had Ris's father lived, the affair Ris had with Helene would never have flowered. And, if it had, she would have been dead long before now."

Part of the guilt was for Ris, as well. Kettwig knew he had sometimes been the only source of warmth for the boy as he grew into early manhood. But the new order was more important than Ris's momentary wants. There was a whole world out there ripe for the taking, and the first step would take place in the next two days in Washington, D.C.

Lifting his glass, Kettwig toasted the two dead men in the picture, knowing Rommel would have spit in his face.

6

Johnny Tallin scooped up the receiver of the house phone before it had a chance to ring a second time. "Tallin," he said as he cradled it next to his ear. He shifted in the water bed until he reached a sitting position, fumbling for his cigarettes on the end table. He cracked his eyes open and scanned the clock/radio's digital readout—4:32 a.m. Whoever was calling had better have a good reason for waking him.

"Johnny, are you awake?"

Tallin recognized Patrizio Madrano's voice at once but couldn't figure out why the old man was whispering. "Yes, sir." He flicked the lighter and squinted against the brightness as he lit his cigarette.

"Some bastard just called me on my private line, Johnny, called me and told me he was coming to see me."

Throwing the sheets to one side, Tallin moved off the bed. Keeping the phone clamped to his ear, he one-handed his underwear on and reached for his pants. "This guy say what he wanted?"

Madrano's voice was strained and raspy. "Hell, no. This bastard has my private number. The goddamn IRS don't have my private number. I'm lying here in bed with those goddamn nightmares I been having ever since Adelio got tossed into the slammer, trying to get some shut-eye before it gets dawn, and this asshole calls me. On my private line. That tell you anything?''

"No, sir. It doesn't tell me a thing, but it raises a lot of questions."

"You're a bright boy, Johnny. I always told you that, eh? Your father used to agree with me, God rest his soul. That was why I made sure you got college, you know, 'cause you're such a bright kid."

Tallin pulled on the wrinkled dress shirt that he'd tossed onto the floor hours earlier and draped his shoulder harness over it. He took a Colt Delta Elite 10 mm pistol from under his pillow and checked the clip before holstering it.

"You hear what I'm telling you, Johnny?"

"Yes, sir." As he zipped his pants, Tallin could smell remnants of Gina's perfume on himself, still taste the musk of the sex they had shared. He tried to remember when she'd left, but couldn't. Gina never stayed around long afterward because she was afraid to.

"There's a wise guy out there, Johnny, someone who has my private number. I'm up here, sitting in the dark in my own goddamn house, afraid to turn on a light 'cause I'm afraid this guy's going to put a bullet through my pump. That ain't right, Johnny."

Tallin disregarded the tie he'd discarded earlier and slipped on his jacket to cover the Colt. Then he stepped into a pair of tennis shoes tucked under the bed and laced them up hurriedly, not bothering with socks. The depth of the problem at hand was suddenly sinking in, bringing a surge of adrenaline with it. The guy had Madrano's private phone number. Tallin didn't have it, and he was the Mafia lord's chief of security. Hell, Gina didn't have it, either, and she was the old man's daughter. "Who does he say he belongs to?"

"Nobody. He just called to say he was going to speak with me tonight and let me know he's sitting down the road from the gate. I look out my window, thinking somebody's just fucking with me or something, and I see a car only a little ways from the gate. Just waiting."

Moving carefully, Tallin stepped to the north window of his second-story room and pulled the curtain to one side as he glanced toward the front of the house. He saw the pair of headlights sitting just left of center of the two-lane blacktop that led to Madrano's estate. He couldn't make out the car or the license plate. The guy was using a car phone, but what the hell made him so sure of himself? Patrizio Madrano wasn't exactly enjoying the retirement the newspapers said he was. Even though he was in his late sixties, the old man still had fangs, still controlled a lot of Mob activity in New York. New guys wanting to establish their own territory still came to him to ask permission. Maybe if Adelio, Madrano's only son, hadn't gotten convicted of murder, maybe Madrano would have retired. But Tallin didn't think so. The old man liked having the power he wielded, was addicted to the respect he commanded. Tallin knew the old man had to be livid at the moment. Yet scared at the same time.

"Johnny, you still there?"

"Yes, sir."

"What do you think?"

Tallin let the curtain drop. "I don't know yet."

"What the hell you mean you don't know yet? You're my fucking chief of security. You can't sit there and tell me you don't know yet."

"I don't know yet," Tallin repeated, "but I'm going to find out."

The old man sighed. "Johnny, I'm sorry I yelled at you. You're a good boy. Your father died protecting me when you were just a kid. You're good at what you do, but you're not hard like your old man. You take too many chances, Johnny. I don't want you getting hurt. A few years back, your old man would send a few soldiers out there to.meet this joker and send him home with his head in his hand if he didn't measure up."

"A few years ago was twenty years ago, Mr. Madrano, and things have to be handled a little differently now." Tallin didn't let the old man's anger touch him as he went over his ideas for addressing the situation that had been dropped into his lap.

"You're right, Johnny. I got a mean temper. Your dad told you about that. It used to get me in a lot of trouble. I'm trying to be more mellow in my later years. I don't bounce back from this confrontation bullshit the way I used to. And these new guys I'm constantly tripping over, this new Mafia that don't know how to act or dress or be gentlemen, you never know when one of these guys is going to blow your head off your shoulders just to make a name for himself."

"I know, sir."

"You're a good boy, Johnny. I know you'll take care of me and Gina."

"Yes, sir, but I need to go meet this guy."

"Let me know what you find out as soon as you can."

"Yes, sir."

"And take care of yourself. I know Gina cares for you a lot." The line clicked dead.

Did the old man know about him and Gina? Tallin wondered as he punched in the numbers for the gate security extension. It wouldn't surprise him if Madrano did. The old fox was still as alert as hell and, even though it seemed sheer torture to spend the days apart, he and Gina didn't get together very often. The old man had never named a heir after Adelio was sent away, never named a chief executor to manage the family business until Adelio got out. If he got out. Was it because he had someone in mind? And was the guy's name Johnny Tallin? Tallin shook his head as he heard the phone ring at the other end. Things were already confused enough trying to honor his father's sense of loyalty to Patrizio Madrano and honor his own debt to the old Mafia lord for the education he had given him. His love for Gina Madrano had only complicated things further. He pushed the thoughts away.

"Yeah?"

"Mike, it's Johnny."

"I was just thinking about calling you, Johnny. We got, maybe, a problem."

"How long's the car been there?"

"You know about that?"

"It's what I get paid all those big bucks for, Mike."

"Terrific. Wait until you're still getting paid all those big bucks lying in a hospital bed with hoses running in and out of you, staring at the ceiling and wondering if you're going to catch the next episode of *The Young and the Restless*."

"How long?"

"About fifteen minutes."

"How many occupants?"

"One."

"Any ID on him?"

"Can't even promise you it's a him, Johnny. The windows are so goddamn polarized you can't see inside."

"Mr. Madrano said it was a guy."

"How the hell would the old man know?"

"The guy called him on his private line and said he wanted to see him."

"Shit."

"Yeah. You or Bobby made any effort at contacting the guy?"

"I sent Bobby out there a few minutes ago to see if it was somebody who just got lost. Before he could get close to the car, it rolled away from him. When he came back to the gate, the car rolled up again."

"I'll be there in a minute, and when I get there I want the guy's plates run and I want to know the car phone number." Tallin hung up and left the room.

He felt cold and edgy as he trotted down the carpeted winding staircase. What kind of guy would have the balls this guy was showing? How many men had Madrano had killed over the years for showing this kind of disrespect?

Karl, the night doorman, pushed himself out of the recliner beside the staircase as Tallin hit the floor. "What's up, chief?" the man asked in his thick Cajun accent.

"Maybe nothing," Tallin replied as he strode to the door, "but watch your ass just the same. Nobody goes in or out of this door unless I okay it."

"You got it, Johnny."

Tallin heard the locks click into place behind him as he moved toward the garage. Ignoring the selection of cars inside the building, he turned and lost himself in the carefully spaced trees covering the estate, making his way through the shadows to the gate house. Security lights cut blue-white swaths through the early-morning darkness with a collection of bugs at each one looking like miniature comets locked in some erratic orbit.

He rapped on the back door of the gate house, saw the peephole go dark for an instant, then stepped back as the door swung out. Mike Blackmon's iron-tough bulk dwarfed the security chief's slender build as he walked inside.

"What do you have?" Tallin asked as he waved away the chair Blackmon offered. He peered through the one-way glass of the gate house, staring into the twin beams of the waiting car. What kind of nerveless bastard was sitting behind the steering wheel? Didn't the guy know there was enough firepower around the estate that would ensure he didn't penetrate the mansion's defenses? And if the guy meant harm, why the hell come head-on like this?

"Got the car's registration and car phone number like you wanted, Johnny," Blackmon said. He waggled a finger at the other man inside the gate house.

Tallin watched Bobby Carloni shift on the small metal desk and take a piece of paper from a pad under the house extension. Carloni and Blackmon were a mis-matched pair. The old and the new, Tallin couldn't help but think every time he saw the men together—Black-mon, older and bulky with knotted muscles and a pen-chant for revolvers, who resentfully stepped into the automatic pistol Tallin had ordered for him, and Car-loni, younger and blond, thin and sallow-faced with an affinity for computer dialogue and programming, who had been only too glad when Tallin upgraded the cur-rent computer Madrano had on hand.

Tallin scanned the paper and asked, "Where'd you get this?"

"DMV, but they don't know that," Carloni answered with a shy smile that hid the killer Tallin knew the man to be.

"Herman, P. W.," Tallin read. Then he checked the mobile phone number. "And the phone?"

"Ma Bell," Carloni replied, flexing his fingers in front of him like cat's claws. "Though the system put up a hell of a fight. That number's new, just like the car, and was restricted. If we didn't keep someone on the pad there for the latest access codes, I couldn't have found it out."

"Who's it registered to?"

Carloni's smile turned into a smirk. "Herman, P. W., same as the car."

"Bastard's got some sense of humor, Johnny. He's sitting out there in a brand-new Ferrari in the middle of the last place he should be and he wants us to think he's Pee-Wee Herman," Blackmon said.

Tallin tapped the paper thoughtfully as he looked back out at the dark bulk of the car. "How new are the car and phone?"

"Two, three hours at the most," Carloni answered.

"Can you track anything farther back on this guy?"

"No. Any information on this guy dead-ends two or three hours ago. I'd have to have his birthdate to track him through the police computers."

"Let me have the phone."

Blackmon handed over the handset, and Tallin punched in the number. The voice that answered was deep, tightly controlled, threatening under a thin veil of civility. "Yeah?"

"Johnny Tallin."

"You're not the guy I want to see."

"I'm the guy you're going to see before you see anybody else." Tallin felt a chill creep down his spine, knowing it was produced by the tone of authority in the unknown man's voice.

"The old man's got cold feet, right?"

"The old man didn't get to be old by being stupid."

"How do you want to handle this?"

"Meet me at the gate house."

"I'm not leaving the car. Madrano's got a lot of reason to be nervous right now, and I'm not about to step into a line of fire."

Tallin was silent, wondering what to do. The guy was too cocksure of himself to come in empty-handed, too alone to be a cop on some kind of bust.

"I know about Kirby Howell, Johnny. The guys Madrano hired missed the hit on Howell in D.C. I'm here on Family business."

"Who are you?"

"A guy, Johnny. A guy who's getting tired of sitting out here."

"What do you know about Howell?"

"Not enough. That's why I'm here to see the old man. People on the Witness program are dropping dead like flies. Some concerned Family heads asked me to check it out."

Asked? Tallin turned it over in his head. Who the hell would be asked by any Family to do anything? Unless the guy commanded some kind of respect. And the guy with the graveyard voice had said Family heads. More than one.

"Come on, Johnny, I don't have all night."

"I'm coming out," Tallin said with more conviction than he felt, "and I'm wearing my gun."

"That's fine, Johnny," the stranger replied. "I'll wear mine, too."

The line clicked dead.

"You can't be serious about going out there, Johnny," Blackmon protested.

Tallin handed him the phone. "Yeah, I am. There's something about this guy, Mike, but I can't put my finger on it."

Tallin let himself out the back way and told Blackmon to secure the door. He felt the darkness of the New York night close starlessly over him as he walked into the twin beams of the sports car with his hands out away from his body. The Colt Delta Elite was lodged in Bianchi break-away leather, and he was confident he could get to it quickly despite the jacket. As he tried to peer through the dark glass of the car, he attempted to put it together in his mind. He knew about the Howell hit, and even protested it to the degree he was entitled to, warning the old man about working outside the Family. Sure, protocol had dropped off considerably since the Bolan days had thinned out a lot of the old blood, but there still existed a lot of the framework that had brought the Families from the old country. And there had been other reasons, as well. Since he'd become head of security two years ago, he hadn't sanctioned any executions and only operated in a retaliatory manner to save Madrano's life or preserve someone else closely linked to the old man. There was no innocent blood on Johnny Tallin's hands, and he wanted to keep it that way.

Yet this guy who had appeared from nowhere with more information than he should have was going to challenge that.

Tallin stopped in front of the car, barely able to distinguish the man in the dark interior. A window hummed down, and the soft tones of a radio playing contemporary music wafted on the still night air.

"Get in, Johnny," the stone-cold voice ordered.

Tallin moved around to the passenger side of the car and opened the door. He slid in, wary for any movement on the other man's part that might signal hostility.

The man was dressed in black, melding into the dark interior of the car, vanishing against the polarized windows. The smell of new leather, from the bucket seats and the short-waisted jacket the man wore, tickled Tallin's nose, and he had to stifle the urge to sneeze. The guy wore dark sunglasses over bronzed skin and showed no emotion as he stared back.

"Who are you?" Tallin asked, surprised at how loud his voice sounded in the confines of the car.

"A guy doing an errand."

"I don't buy that."

The stranger grinned, and Tallin was surprised at the warmth it contained. "I wouldn't, either, Johnny."

"So what do you want?"

"To talk to Madrano."

"About the Howell thing?"

"About who he hired to do the Howell hit."

"If you know so much, why don't you know who did the hit?"

Mack Bolan moved his cuff to glance at his watch. "I was told you were a smart guy, Johnny. I wish I had the time to examine the length and breadth of all that intellect, but I'm a busy man and the numbers on this one are falling fast. I'm about two steps ahead of a federal agency, and I want to keep it that way."

"I don't think Mr. Madrano wants to talk to you, which means we've got a problem."

"He's going to talk to me," Bolan replied calmly, "because he doesn't have a choice."

Tallin took out his cigarettes and started to light up. "As long as I'm here, he has a choice."

"Put the cigarettes away."

Tallin glanced at the guy, stung by the force of the command.

"Look, Johnny, I don't mean to make your life hard, and I don't mean to deprive you of a smoke, but if I were you, I would have stationed a guy with a sniper scope inside the gate house and told him to take out the driver of this car when he lit a cigarette and cast some light on things. You understand?''

Nodding, Tallin put the cigarette and lighter in a pocket. This guy was definitely one cagey customer.

''Madrano will see me. Just tell him I have this.'' Bolan handed him a flat rectangle.

Tallin took it, shifting in his seat to take advantage of the illumination from the car stereo controls. When he saw the black ace of spades, he felt a shiver ripple through him. A Black Ace. One of the enforcement arm that settled inter-Family disputes, with the power to execute a Mafia don of even Madrano's stature without being held accountable for the action. He had heard Madrano and his father talk about the men in fear and awe. When he looked back at the guy, the easy smile was back in place.

''Give the old man a call, Johnny, and see what he says. I'm willing to bet we don't have any more problems. Here, use my phone. I have the number.'' He handed Tallin the phone.

After punching in the number, Tallin looked at the mansion, staring at the dark window that belonged to Madrano and wondering how much trouble the old man was in, wondering, too, what he would do if the guy sitting next to him had come to execute Gina's father.

7

Bolan followed Johnny Tallin into Patrizio Madrano's fortress, aware that at least half a dozen hardmen had stepped into position somewhere behind him. Aware, also, that if he didn't play his cards right, he'd be a dead man. But according to the rules the Mafia don played by, an ace of spades couldn't be beaten. And Bolan intended to live the role of the Ace to the hilt during his interview with the man.

Under the supervision of the Taliaferro brothers, Pat and Mike, the Aces had come into legendary power among the Families in their ability to finalize whatever disputes came to their attention. Madrano had been around long enough to know better than to question a Black Ace who appeared before him. That Bolan was allowed entrance to the house was proof of that. But the threat, the image, of the force he purported to be, that had to remain constant in the old man's eyes, or blood would be spilled.

Dressed as he was in the black leather jacket and matching gloves, black slacks and black turtleneck, Bolan knew he'd fulfill Madrano's visual expectations. The swagger, the superciliousness, the ego, those he'd deliver in the way he moved and in the way he talked.

Johnny Tallin hadn't said a word since speaking with the old man over the car phone and had instinctively taken the lead when guiding Bolan to his boss. According to Kurtzman's files on the security chief, Tallin had blood ties linking him deeply to the old Mafia that had been smashed by the Executioner's onslaught in past years. But he seemed to be turned in a different direction. Tallin's record was clean, even after serving as Madrano's head of security. From intel gleaned from FBI files, Tallin was drug-free and remained his own man.

Bolan saw Tallin wave the doorman to one side, then followed the younger man up the winding staircase. How many other men were inside the house? Bolan figured the numbers would steadily increase the whole time he talked with Madrano, and hoped the security chief could keep the guns in line.

Tallin paused at a door at the end of the hallway and rapped softly.

"Johnny?"

Bolan recognized the old man's voice from their earlier conversation on the phone.

"It's me, Mr. Madrano."

"You alone, Johnny?"

"No, sir."

"Let me see the card."

Tallin looked at Bolan expectantly. Bolan gave him the card, regulating him to his continued role as messenger. Tallin took it and slid it under the door.

Looking at the expensively faked veneer of the wood, Bolan figured that nothing less than steel plate swung on the ornate hinges. There was a momentary pause while the card disappeared, and Tallin's eyes never left Bolan's face.

"You recognize this guy, Johnny?" Madrano asked.

"No, sir. He's had plastic surgery."

Bolan gave him a thin grin, impressed that Tallin had noticed the minute, telltale signs left from the high-quality work the government had paid for the last time he'd gone under the knife, when he had joined the Phoenix program.

Bolan addressed the door, keeping his eyes on Tallin. "If I had all night to talk to you, Madrano, I would have come in the morning and saved us both some sleep. I've got a lot of things to secure between now and morning, and cooling my heels here isn't going to get them done."

"In my time," Madrano said, "a young man knew how to respect his elders."

"Even in my time," Bolan snapped, "it was a matter of respect to keep Family business within the Family."

A lock clicked back in the door, followed by two more.

"Let him in, Johnny, and come in yourself."

"Yes, sir." Tallin pushed the door open and allowed Bolan to precede him.

Bolan didn't hesitate, knowing an Ace would recognize the respect due him in this situation and show no fear of the security chief.

The door opened into a lavishly furnished anteroom rather than the bedroom Bolan had expected. Expensive curtains covered ornate windows, falling to Persian carpet, draping hand-tooled furniture done in rich golden brown wood. The lighting was soft and left scattered shadows in the room. It was a room built to contain whispers and illicit business transactions.

Patrizio Madrano sat in a wheelchair near the center of the room, looking like an old and bald lizard draped in a monogrammed maroon robe. A gray blanket covered the thin legs that had been useless since a sniper's bullet had paralyzed the old man ten years ago. The wheelchair was motorized, and hummed as Madrano powered it backward so that he wouldn't have to lift his head as high to look at Bolan.

The warrior surveyed the room while Tallin locked the door behind him.

"You got a name, wise guy?" Madrano asked. His head bobbed uncertainly on the skinny stalk of a neck.

"Omega," Bolan replied. It was a name that had served him before when passing through inner sanctums of the Mafia on intelligence-gathering forays.

"What kind of name is that?" Madrano demanded.

"It's not a name," Tallin said from behind Bolan. "It's a letter from the Greek alphabet. It translates loosely as 'the end.'"

Madrano grinned at Bolan. "How about that, Mr. High and Mighty Black Ace? I ain't just your run-of-the-mill dago wop who figures a Thompson is the sure way to the top of the heap. I surround myself with guys like Johnny there to make sure I get a well-rounded view of the world."

"A smart guy like you should know better than to screw around with Family business, then," Bolan said in an icy voice.

The old man's face reddened. "You don't have any class at all, Omega. Anybody ever tell you that before?"

"I don't have any time, Madrano. This fuck-up you made in D.C. is blowing the lid off something that's leading right back to you and to a lot of other people."

Madrano gripped the wheels of the chair angrily, rolling himself forward. "Who the hell are you to come into my house and give me this kind of crap?"

"You got my card right there in your lap. You tell me who I am."

"One word from me, and Johnny will take the back of your head off."

Bolan could feel the tension in the room. For a moment he read his death in the withered features of the old man.

Then the fury dropped away from Madrano, and he rolled the chair backward again. "It wasn't my fuck-up in the beginning."

Bolan nodded. "I know that, but the Feds are going to track this thing directly to you. Kirby Howell escaped the hit team you hired, and one of their wounded spilled your name. Chances are there's a federal warrant being issued right now with your name on it."

"What do you want from me?"

"I need to know who you hired to make the hit on Howell."

Using his arms, Madrano shifted in the wheelchair. "Would it surprise you to know that I don't *know* who I hired?"

Bolan didn't reply, letting his silence push Madrano into an avenue of explanation.

"There was a guy who got in touch with me through my lawyer," the old man said. "Told my mouthpiece he knew where this black guy was hiding out and could do him. If the price was right. Of course, I didn't believe him. Told him to take a flying fuck at the moon. I figured it was some kind of Fed trick, some kind of entrapment thing. I been putting up with this shit ever since Adelio got put in the slammer. There must be twenty of those yuppie twits in the IRS office going over every return I ever filed." The old man looked away from Bolan. "They figure now that they got Adelio where they want him, that I'll roll over on some of the Family to save my son. I've got these little mystery calls from people I don't know who tell me my son's enjoying his new black boyfriend, that he's getting to be a real hit in the shower.

I can't even leave my house to go see Adelio because some young hot-blooded turks want to make a name for themselves by trying to take me out. So I sit here in this goddamn house, thinking about my boy and the hell he must be going through, wanting to do something but not knowing what." The burning eyes centered on Bolan again, red-rimmed with barely contained emotion. "Then I got you, Mr. Black Ace, coming up here to put me on some kind of trial for wanting to make things a little more even for my boy."

Bolan let the silence hang uncertainly for a moment, knowing it was a father's love he confronted, backed by Mafia power. Maybe, if he hadn't read the files on Patrizio Madrano's "boy," the old man's passion and sense of loss would have touched him. But he had spent too many years fighting men like them, men who knew no compassion unless it touched their own ranks. "What about the guy you hired?"

Madrano glared at him. "Is it true, Mr. Black Ace, that when they recruit you guys they pour ice water in your veins and make you eat your own heart?"

Bolan made himself smirk. "They don't make us do the heart thing anymore."

"Fuck you, wise guy. Fuck you and the guys who sent you." Madrano powered the chair in a one-eighty and rolled forward to come to rest by the window.

"Madrano," Bolan said forcefully, "I didn't come here tonight to take your head back in a basket. I was told to get information."

"I don't have any information. Haven't you been listening? These guys, they sent me some pictures of Howell, pictures of him since the court days. I could tell they were real from the background, from the way this black looked, but I couldn't tell where he was. Otherwise I would have had my own guys do it, and there wouldn't have been any fuck-ups. Just one dead, bigmouthed black bastard. My mouthpiece arranged a meet.''

"Where?''

"Here.''

"This guy trusted you that much?''

"I didn't give him a choice. If he wanted to work for me, then he would meet me here, on my ground.''

Bolan wondered about that briefly. Why would anyone from the team take a chance on being identified later if they went to the lengths they did to remain unknown on the Howell operation? "Then what happened?''

"I hired him to hit Howell.''

"This guy leave a name or an address where you could send the money?''

"No. I paid him up front.''

"The whole amount?''

"Yeah, yeah, so you can go back to whoever you report to and tell them Patrizio Madrano is going senile as well as soft. But this guy left you with that impression, you know, of being able to do what he said. He had pictures of this guy, who I couldn't even find in the years I had people looking. And other guys I talked to, the ones this guy suggested I contact before making any decisions, they said these hitters could make good on their delivery.''

"Who else besides Scorscini used them?'' Bolan asked.

When the chair creaked back around again, there was a sad half smile on Madrano's face. "What you want I should do, Mr. Black Ace, start rolling over on people now so you guys know you're right? No. You're so fucking smart, you find out those names yourself. And if that ain't good enough, you can shoot me here and take your chances with Johnny.''

"You never got a name from this man who met with you?"

"No. He was a salesman hawking a bill of goods. He didn't need no name, not even a Halloween one like Omega or whatever the hell you're calling yourself."

"You didn't try to trace him?"

"Why? For the money? I got more money than I need. My son is what I need. Revenge is what I need."

"What did this man look like?"

"You figure on bumping into him?"

"Maybe. He needs to be told not to poke his nose into Family business."

"Maybe if the Families took care of each other, there wouldn't be nobody buttin' in."

Bolan remained silent, staring at the man through the dark sunglasses.

Abruptly Madrano broke the eye contact. "He was redheaded, a big guy like you, fair skin, so I know he was no *paisan*. The limo that brought him was rented, and the name and address he left with the company dead-ended. That's all I know. The guy came here, showed his pictures and left. If you want any more information, you'll have to ask somebody else."

Nodding, Bolan said, "Someone will be in touch with you."

Madrano gave him a tight grin. "I won't hold my breath." He lifted a finger to indicate the door. "Johnny, show the man out. Make sure no one takes his disrespect toward me personally."

Bolan followed Tallin out. A man with an automatic rifle faded into another room at the security man's wave.

"How much trouble is the old man in?" Tallin asked as they went down the stairs.

"It's not up to me," Bolan replied truthfully, thinking of the Mafia Commission and the Justice people, as well. They'd be in touch with Madrano by morning, after everything Turrin knew hit the intelligence circuit.

"He tried to help you," Tallin pointed out. "He told you everything he knew."

"How do you know?"

"I checked these guys out for him. There was nothing."

"You advised him to go ahead with this?"

Tallin shook his head. "I advised against it, but he didn't listen. Adelio wasn't much, and I know how much trouble I could be in for telling you that if it gets back to Mr. Madrano, but he was all the old man had in the way of passing on his business."

"Where do you figure in this?" Bolan asked as they stepped through the front doors.

"I like the old man. At least the part of him that he shows to me when we're alone. He treats me right. And I have other reasons."

Bolan looked at the security chief, sensing more depth behind Tallin's words, knowing at the same time that now wasn't the time to press the issue. He started to turn away, then felt his combat senses flare to sudden life. Something. A bright flickering at the top of the tree line on the other side of the estate walls. He reacted instinctively, twisting to one side as he pushed Tallin down with an outstretched arm. Bullets scattered brick dust from the wall where they had been standing.

Then he was rolling away from the lights, moving toward the sheltered darkness around the parking area. The Beretta was in his hands as he flipped over onto his back the second time, its 9 mm slugs shattering the porch lights. He gathered his legs under him as he scanned the tree line again.

"Tallin?"

"I'm okay. Thanks."

Bolan glanced over his shoulder and saw that the younger man was already on his feet, tucked out of sight behind the low brick wall that led to the garage area.

Startled shouts came from the gate house, and return fire raked the treetops.

Orange muzzle-flashes winked in three different areas of the trees, and the front of the house became a hotbed of flying lead. Keeping low behind the brick wall, Bolan duck-walked toward the Ferrari, keeping the 93-R fisted in his hand in case any of the attackers had penetrated the estate's security. His mind rejected the possibility of Mob activity. As old as Madrano was, the dons of the other Families would wait for the man's death by natural causes, then split the territory however they had already decided. No, this scanned as something else entirely.

"Who the hell is it?" Tallin asked.

"I'm guessing it's part of the group Madrano hired to hit Howell."

"But why?"

"That I don't know," Bolan replied. How much manpower did the group have? What kind of connections did they have that allowed them to come and go so easily? Why were they so willing to expend that manpower in an effort to keep Patrizio Madrano from telling him anything when the man had nothing to tell? Bolan came to a stop at the end of the wall, looking back at the darkened trees and wondering if the snipers were still there, wondering if he could make it to the sports car before a withering burst of autofire cut him down.

"You going after those guys?" Tallin asked.

"Yeah."

"Make sure the passenger door is unlocked when you get inside then," Tallin said, "because you aren't going alone."

"These guys aren't amateurs, Johnny. They've walked the hellgrounds, not the concrete sidewalks where most of the Family tough guys make their bones."

Tallin grinned. "I'm not reacting out of some threatened macho ego, Omega, and I'm not trying to put on some dog-and-pony show for you. I spent three years in the Green Berets before I took my college degree. I'm not going to be a liability, and I'm damn good in the dark. Now, are we going to continue this debate, or are we going after those guys?"

"We're going," Bolan said grimly, wondering at the whims of fate that sided him with this likable Mafia security chief. He threw himself into an all-out sprint for the sports car, diving across the hood as if he were sliding into second base. Pulling the door open, he slid behind the wheel, keyed the ignition and thumbed up the electric lock on the passenger door. A breathless Tallin was beside him seconds later.

Bolan threw the sports car in reverse and, leaving the lights off, heeled the car across the parking area to take advantage of the darker gloom of the lawn. Bullets spit flame from the driveway, chewing up a limousine parked beside his last position. He watched Tallin dial a number on the car phone as he cut the wheel hard and found first gear. The back tires slipped and chewed clumps from the expensively manicured lawn as they sought traction. The rear end of the car spun free, then settled down into a low-set trajectory for the front gate.

"Blackmon, it's Johnny," Tallin said as he struggled to keep himself in the seat. "Open the goddamn gate and alert the security teams." Then he threw the receiver onto the floor.

Bolan blew through the gate without pausing, hearing the rasp of metal against metal as the gate gouged the side of the sports car. He raked the sunglasses from his face, and they joined the receiver. He held the Beretta in his left hand, muzzle resting lightly on the side mirror.

"If possible, I want one of these guys in one piece to answer some questions."

"No promise," Tallin replied.

Bolan nodded. He overcontrolled the car, sending it into a sideways spin that tracked him back onto the side road he had come up earlier. A figure darted from the thick woods ahead of the vehicle, beelining to the center of the road. The M-16 in the man's hands drilled a series of holes through the passenger side of the windshield, showering Tallin with fragments of glass.

The Executioner bore down on the assassin before the man had another chance to aim his weapon. Bolan felt the anger in the man's eyes burning into his face seconds before the sports car slammed into him. The assassin flipped over the hood, shattering his face against Bolan's windshield before sliding off the car and onto the road.

Seconds later a dark van equipped with four-wheel drive shot out of the wooded area behind him, locking onto the rear of the Ferrari. Realizing he had been outflanked, the Executioner jammed his foot hard on the accelerator.

"Sucker play," Tallin said.

"Classic," Bolan agreed.

"I don't read this as an attempt on Madrano anymore."

"Neither do I," Bolan replied without elaborating. He had enough questions of his own without resolving any that Tallin had. How had these guys tracked him and why? What did they think he knew about them? He pushed the questions away, striving to remember the lay of the road as they raced through the darkness. The Delta Elite Johnny Tallin wielded with grim efficiency popped occasionally in his ear, numbing his hearing. There was no doubt the sports car could easily outdistance the assassins, but that wouldn't put him any closer to discovering who they were. He had been on the fringes of the operation when he had linked up with Turrin. The attack on him now put him smack in the middle. With no understanding of why. By rights the group should have been pursuing Leo. But since Turrin was out of reach at Stony Man Farm, it was possible that Bolan had been their only option. Maybe they hadn't followed him at all. Maybe they had put the Madrano estate under observation after the bungled Howell hit in order to see who crawled out of the woodwork. Someone could have recognized him, or he matched the description of the other surviving assassins.

Bolan yanked the steering wheel hard left, and the vehicle swerved in a sudden, tire-eating turn. He glanced in the rearview mirror, easing up on the accelerator to allow the van to gain on them momentarily. When the first handful of shots cracked into the rear of the sports car, he tromped on the accelerator, pulling away from the van easily.

"Get ready," Bolan told Tallin as he checked the rearview mirror again. "We're going to be EVA in a couple of minutes."

"Going to sacrifice the car?" the security chief asked.

"Yeah." Losing sight of the van's headlights over the last hill he passed, Bolan braked hard and heard rubber scream in agony. He cut the wheel, pushing the car into a sideways slide that covered most of the road. Then he was out of the vehicle, moving for the side of the road. He watched Tallin take up position on the opposite side, melding into the darkness.

The van topped the rise, and the high-intensity fog lights picked up the car at once. For a moment it looked as if the driver might maintain enough control over the van to miss the car by going off the road on Bolan's side. Then the right side of the van glanced off the front end of the car, and they spun in a death embrace of tortured metal. The van flipped over onto its side, rolling only yards from the Executioner's position.

Bolan was in motion before the vehicle came to rest. The back doors squeaked open, and an assassin stepped out, holding his M-16 at shoulder level. Autofire lanced through the brush to the Executioner's left. The Beretta coughed out a silenced 3-round burst that blew the gunner back inside the vehicle.

Holding the Beretta at the ready and moving in a semicrouch, the Executioner made his way carefully to the front of the overturned vehicle.

A body lay half in and half out of the shattered windshield. The unnatural angle of the man's neck told Bolan that he wouldn't be getting up again. There was no one else in the cab of the van.

Bolan walked to the rear of the vehicle and hauled out the body of the gunner he'd shot. Tallin reached the vehicle at a dead run.

"You okay?" the security chief asked.

Bolan nodded as he started to empty the dead man's pockets.

"Damn, you move fast."

"Too fast," Bolan said. "I should have left this guy intact."

"From where I was, I didn't see that he left you any choice."

"Maybe not," Bolan agreed. There was nothing in the man's pockets except spare clips for the M-16. The warrior moved up front again with Tallin in tow, seeking the vehicle's registration. There was a name on the papers that Bolan didn't recognize. He guessed Kurtzman's computers would encounter the same thing unless someone had elaborated on a false identity that would require man-hours to check out. He slipped the registration inside his jacket pocket just the same. If the false trails kept adding up, maybe there would be something in them that would help triangulate the enemy's real location. "Do you recognize any of these guys?"

Tallin shook his head. "No, but seeing this guy in the back reminded me of something."

Bolan followed him to the rear of the vehicle.

Tallin knelt and picked up the dead man's left arm. "This tattoo," the security chief said. "The guy who pitched the deal to the old man had one of these on his arm, too."

Bolan studied it. The tattoo was on the inside of the forearm, closer to the elbow than the wrist, detailing some kind of hawk presented in profile with its wings askew, one forward and one backward as if it were swimming rather than flying. "You're sure?" he asked Tallin.

"Yeah. You don't see something like this every day. I figured it for some kind of military thing, but I didn't know who."

Lights flared over the top of the road as a limousine wheeled into view. The driver was barely able to avoid the wrecked Ferrari.

"My guys," Tallin announced as they stood up together.

Bolan nodded. "Get somebody on this. I want the local police kept out as much as possible, and I want you to find out what you can about these guys and that tattoo." He glanced back at the dead man's arm, knowing he had no choice about the orders he had given the security chief. An Ace wouldn't have wanted outside interference in Family business. Hell, that was what he was supposed to be seeing Madrano about. And he doubted whether the local law-enforcement agencies would have as much access to intel as Tallin did. A Family as old as Patrizio Madrano's would have information-gathering tentacles spread in many areas, and more than a few most agencies wouldn't be able to reference. Maybe they could come up with another piece of the puzzle.

"Anything else?" Tallin asked as they walked back to the road.

"Yeah." Bolan holstered the Beretta and looked at the twisted wreckage of the sports car. "It looks like I could use a ride."

8

A spotty cloud cover hung threateningly over the Washington, D.C., area when the Stony Man jet touched down. After securing a rental car using the Belasko identity, Bolan placed a call to Kurtzman on an outside pay phone. He turned up the collar on his leather jacket as protection against the drifting mist that swirled across the airport while he waited for the connection to be made.

Kurtzman answered on the third ring.

"Aaron?"

"That you, Mack?"

"Yeah. I took the chance you might still be up."

"I was going over some of the stuff we turned up tonight, making sure there wasn't anything we'd overlooked. I've also been running a little interference and gathering information for Hal. He's still at the scene of the office building hit where you and Leo kicked the ball into play. Security nets are tightening all over the city."

"The Russians have been informed of the situation?"

"Yeah, but the meet is still on. Gorbachev and the Man agree that too much time and too much publicity have already been put into this thing to back out now."

"But it's going to be a hell of a tense situation while they're here."

"I'd say that was a safe bet."

Bolan studied the dark clouds sweeping the pale yellow moon from sight and wondered if they might be serving as some kind of omen. He was certain there was more to the recent murders in D.C. than just killing for hire. Maybe there wasn't any factual evidence that proved it, but the present state of affairs grated against the keen edge of his warrior's senses. Why go into business in D.C. now, when security was sure to be the most restricted? The hits themselves came too quickly on the heels of one another, as well. There had to be another team that negotiated the transactions in order to allow the strike team free time to set up the termination. It would have been interesting to find out how many of the hits were actually sanctioned by Family members, and if any of them had been done for nothing. So, yeah, considering all of the factors that chafed at his finely tuned strategist's mind, he felt sure he had only touched the tip of the iceberg on an operation much more critical than just a very efficient merc team operating within the boundaries of the nation's capital.

"Mack?"

"Yeah, Aaron. I was just turning some things over in my mind."

"And found out it was totally unproductive, right?"

"For the moment."

"That's what I've been getting on this end."

"I came across something at Madrano's that might lead somewhere, though." Quickly Bolan outlined the events that had taken place at the mafioso's estate, describing the tattoo in detail. When he finished, he asked, "Does the tattoo ring a bell in your mind?"

"I can't place it, but then I don't have the military background you have."

"I don't know if it fits into the military yet," Bolan said. "I haven't been able to place it if it does. Unless it's something new that one of the specialized branches has started."

"Then why should it ring any bells with me?"

"Because you've seen it. Do you still have Dwight Hooker's file?"

"Yeah."

"Punch it up onto your screen and flip through the pictures on Hooker doing civic duty. The third or fourth photograph. The one where Hooker is talking to the kids at a local Just-Say-No chapter."

"Got it."

"Do you see it?"

"I don't even know what I'm looking for." Kurtzman sounded puzzled.

"Use the image enhancer and blow up Hooker's left forearm. In that position the inside of the arm will be presented to you." Bolan waited, fixing the image in his own mind. He was pretty confident of what he remembered, but he wanted Kurtzman's affirmative.

"Son of a gun," Kurtzman said hoarsely. "I completely missed that."

"I didn't catch it, either, until I was on the jet back here. And I wasn't completely sure it was there until now."

"It's the same bird you described to me, right? Presented profile with the wings bent like it's windmilling or something?"

"That's the one."

"So now we have a tie between the hitters and the bug that was placed on your car. But why would they be interested in you? As far as anyone knows, you're attached solely to the security team protecting Gorbachev and his entourage.''

"Curiouser and curiouser," Bolan said wryly.

Kurtzman grumped. "But instead of narrowing the question of who these guys are, this has only opened up more possibilities.''

"As well as stepping up the urgency on this thing.''

"Yeah, Hal's going to be real happy to find out about this.''

Bolan wiped collected moisture from his face with a big hand. Behind him the windshield wipers on the rented car swacked out a slow metronome. "Let me add a new wrinkle. Check Hooker's police record.''

"Got it.''

"Is there any mention of the tattoo?''

"No, which means the guy got it after he joined the force.''

"Right. It might be interesting to find out when he got it if we can. It could possibly correlate a few other things.''

"I'll still check on the military angle, though. This operation seems too well organized to not have those connections somewhere.''

"Agreed," Bolan said. "When you go through your files, check on American paramilitary groups as well as whatever we have on those operating out of European theaters.''

"I've got a guy in Europe I can reach tonight who might be able to turn us onto something if these jokers are coming from that direction.''

"I don't think the team lives there," Bolan said as he considered what Johnny Tallin had told him earlier. "These guys fit in too easily to the American way of life. They know a lot of behind-the-scenes crime stats, some of them years old. This isn't a fly-by-night project. But there may be some European financing.''

Kurtzman sighed, and Bolan could hear the big man's chair squeak as it shifted. ''The thing that bothers me is why someone has initiated this operation now. If it's going to be a play against the Prez and Gorbachev, how can they hope to succeed with all the security involved in this meeting?''

''I don't know,'' Bolan replied. He shifted and felt cold water run down his back under the jacket.

''Hal wanted me to ask you when you were planning on showing up this morning.''

''Tell him I'll be there in plenty of time to help with the security situation.''

''Okay.''

Bolan shrugged inside the jacket, feeling the wet spot between his shoulders as he resettled the combat harness. Then he asked for Dwight Hooker's home address.

BOLAN LEFT the rental car parked at the curb two buildings down from his objective. He crossed the sidewalk and claimed the shadows that still hugged the walls of the apartment building complex.

He made his way through an open breezeway, maneuvering around kids' bikes, patio furniture and charcoal grills. The swimming pool in the center of the complex was a shallow kidney shape whose surface rippled slightly with the light rain that had followed the Executioner into Fairfax.

Morning noises echoed around him as he moved— television voices covering the day's agenda of news so that the viewers would be better informed, and grumpy, low-pitched voices of parents as they carried on conversations in an attempt to keep from waking the children.

Bolan stepped out of the breezeway and headed for Dwight Hooker's building at an oblique angle, staying away from the windows. According to what Kurtzman had been able to pull from the files, Hooker lived alone in a second-floor apartment, number 23920.

The Executioner walked through the small curtain of rain leaking from the upper walls of the building. He reached inside the jacket and touched the butt of the Beretta, making sure the breakaway holster was positioned correctly for a fast draw.

He took the metal stairs leading up to the second floor of the neighboring building, taking care to move quietly. A door opened at the end of the hallway, sending Bolan's hand streaking for his gun. He checked the motion immediately when he saw a guy step from the apartment carrying a metal lunch box and a red thermos. Bolan gave the man a friendly nod as they passed in the breezeway.

After the man had disappeared from sight, the warrior braced himself against the wall and stepped up on the black metal railing at the edge of the building. He gripped the eave in both gloved hands and arced his body to the rooftop.

He remained prone for a moment, letting the shadows absorb him as he got his bearings. Dwight Hooker's building was to his left. The smell of wet tar clogged his nostrils, and the odor of wood burning in a fireplace wafted to him on a slight breeze.

Keeping low, Bolan moved toward his target, stopping at the edge of the roof. Air-conditioning units pulsed a steady hum behind him as air fans suctioned the exhaust from the building. The shrill screams of a child crying shattered the heartbeat of the normal morning noises, then quickly subsided. The sluggish crank of a starter sounded from the direction of the parking lot, then exploded into a throaty roar as the engine caught.

The lights in Dwight Hooker's apartment were off. Bolan sat in silent contemplation of the target area, trying to get a feel for the place, searching through the sometimes tangled impressions his combat senses relayed to him. Even if reports of the New York attempt hadn't filtered back through whatever chain of command was keeping the merc team together, what were the chances Hooker would be at home now? They couldn't know he had found the bug on the car bumper, but his appearance at the office building hit had to have let them know something had gone awry. So had they assumed Hooker would be untraceable, or had the man been left as bait in a trap?

He scanned the other rooftops, trying to separate the shadows from the tar surfaces. Something tugged at the fringe of his conscious mind, and he used his peripheral vision to make another pass. This time he identified the two snipers lying on rooftops, covering the front of the breezeway that led to Hooker's apartment. The angle of their placement had prevented them from seeing him reach the rooftop.

After mentally marking the snipers' positions, Bolan eased back to the edge of the rooftop in the other direction. He swung back down to the second-story breezeway and dropped quietly to the floor. He moved at a sedate pace in a circle outside the perimeter of the building where one of the men waited.

The warrior used the balcony of the apartment at the back of the building to reach the first man, hauling himself up first one story then the next. He paused at the edge of the rooftop to free the Beretta from its leather, then pushed himself onto the pebbled wet tar surface.

The sniper whirled, flushed from hiding. The big bore rifle cradled loosely in his arms rose like a striking cobra. The weapon cracked and the Executioner could hear the impact as the slug plowed into a nearby wall.

The Beretta, locked in 3-shot mode, coughed twice, six 9 mm hornets exploding into the assassin. The rounds shattered the man's chest, then tracked up toward his face. The corpse fell backward and the rifle clattered to the rooftop.

Bolan threw himself behind the protective bulk of the air-conditioning unit as the sniper on the other rooftop opened up. Metal screamed when the high powered rounds scored through the thin shield protecting the refrigeration unit.

Reaching from behind cover, Bolan snagged the pant leg of the man he'd shot and pulled the body toward him. He whipped the hood of the sniper's black raincoat back and examined the guy's face only to find it unknown to him. He pushed back the sleeve of the man's left arm and found the tattoo.

Shots drummed into the air-conditioning unit in a final burst as the sniper's weapon ran dry. Bolan was in motion at once, flinging himself up and charging forward. He didn't pause at the edge of the roof, grabbing for the outside post of the balcony with his left hand as he let his feet slide over.

A volley of lead thundered through the reinforced sheet metal that covered the balcony area, echoing hollowly across the apartment complex. Bolan felt at least one of the bullets strike the pine four-by-four he hung from by one hand. Gritting his teeth against the roughness of the abrasive wooden surface, the Executioner let himself fall full-length against the balcony railing, then dropped to the ground.

A startled face peered at him frantically from the double glass doors of the lower apartment, then the closing curtains swept it away. Powering his legs like a four-hundred-meter hurdler on an Olympic record run, Bolan sprinted for the other building, hoping to catch the other man before he could make good his escape. He slammed into the wall with his left hand, rolling toward the breezeway as he raised the 93-R to shoulder level.

A man stepped out of an apartment with a confused look on his face. Bolan motioned him back inside. "Police," he announced in an authoritative voice. "Call the Fairfax PD and let them know I need a backup."

The man nodded and quickly vanished.

Bolan wiped the moisture from his eyes and eyebrows, listening intently. Heavy thumping from overhead echoed inside the breezeway. Hoping the guy would make the phone call to the police department so that the uniforms would know there was a friendly in the war zone, Bolan traced the thumping to the other end of the building. He paused, rainwater sprinkling across his forearms as he held the Beretta in a Weaver's grip.

A muffled curse reached his ears, followed by a loud crash.

Wheeling around the corner of the building, Bolan saw a figure struggling to rise from the shattered remains of a balcony. The thin metal sheeting had evidently given way beneath the sniper's weight and spilled him onto the aluminum furniture below.

The shock of blond hair above the dark raincoat told Bolan that his quarry was Dwight Hooker. Wanting to take the man alive, Bolan leathered the Beretta and raced for the second-story balcony. He hurled himself into the air as Hooker's head snapped around in his direction. His fingers curled around the metal railing, and he struggled to pull himself up.

Hooker found the dropped weapon the same moment Bolan threw a leg over the railing. The man swung up the rifle, and a pair of bullets pulverized the double balcony doors. Glass flew in all directions. Bolan felt something hot-cool touch his chin and knew the trickling warmth on his skin was blood.

Then he was kicking out with both feet as he brought the rest of his body weight across the railing. He hit Hooker in the sternum and felt something break.

Hooker smashed into the railing behind him, and the rifle flew from his hands to the sidewalk below. Growling with rage, the big man rushed the Executioner with balled fists.

There was little room to maneuver. Bolan felt himself carried along with Hooker's rush until he smacked into the restraining metal behind him. A heavy-knuckled fist caught him on his left temple, and for a moment his vision went black.

Hooker's fingers locked around his throat as the bigger man pinned him against the railing and started to bend him backward.

Blood throbbed in Bolan's temples as he fought the other man's strength without the leverage he needed. With agonizing slowness, he curled his spine and forced Hooker back, ignoring the punishing pressure at his throat. Black comets swirled sickeningly before the Executioner's eyes, becoming dark holes that threatened to suck him away.

Once he had position back, Bolan released the railing with his right hand and brought his forearm up and over Hooker's arms, sweeping them away. His left fist darted in and tagged a mouse over the man's right eye. Bolan followed it with another left, then a right to the rib cage as Hooker tried to cover his face. He managed to rock Hooker's head with another combination before the bigger man screamed in sudden fury and tried to duplicate the earlier rush.

Ducking under the man's outswept arms, Bolan grabbed the front of the raincoat and added his impetus to Hooker's, bouncing the man into and over the railing. Without waiting, Bolan flung himself over the side of the balcony as well and landed between Hooker and the rifle.

Hooker tried to get up, but the angle of the man's left leg told Bolan the assassin wouldn't be able to stand even if he could get up. The man's features went pale when the leg grated at the attempt with a sickening sound that reached even Bolan's ears.

Breathing heavily in response to his body's demand for oxygen, Bolan reached under his black leather jacket and pulled the Beretta out where Hooker could see it. He motioned with the barrel. "Hands where I can see them," he commanded. "You know the moves."

"I should have killed you last night," Hooker snarled. "I told them you looked like trouble." His eyes were feverish with pain.

"Who are you working for?" Bolan asked as he walked closer to the man.

"It's not 'who,'" Hooker said. "It's 'what,' and it's something greater than the lives of a few people. Righting an injustice always is."

"What are you talking about?" Images of the gunner blowing himself up at the arcade tumbled through his mind.

"I'm talking about the future, Belasko," Hooker replied. "Your future, if you live that long, and the future of this country. It looks bleak. You're going to see a wolf's winter before the week is out.''

Bolan identified the fanatical gleam in the man's eyes and felt himself tense as he brought the Beretta's trigger pull down to half a pound.

The shrill keening of sirens sliced through the morning stillness.

When he saw Hooker's jaw work suddenly, then clench as he bit into something, Bolan cursed silently and rushed forward. He tucked the 93-R into the shoulder holster and wrapped a hand around the big man's chin as he tried to work Hooker's mouth open. The assassin struggled under him, laughing maniacally.

''You're too late, Belasko,'' the man said triumphantly. His breath was tainted with the odor of bitter almonds. ''I'll be waiting for you in hell.''

Bolan felt the man's body jerk in sudden convulsions and watched as the eyes rolled upward until only the whites showed. The light rain fell on the sightless eyes and they stared without blinking.

Moving off the body, Bolan sat on the wet ground, feeling the tiredness and the killing soak into him with the rain, wondering what the hell it was Hooker had been protecting that would cause the man to give up his life so freely. He rolled the man's left sleeve back to examine the tattoo. The same stylized bird hung there in endless flight, maintaining the same secret it had held for however long it had been in existence.

When the first uniformed cop appeared around the corner, Bolan put his hands on his head as he was instructed.

''Promise me, boy!''
''I promise, Father.''

"You're lying."

"No, Father, I swear it. I promise."

"There is no commitment in your eyes, boy."

"It is in my heart."

"Only because I put it there. I put it there but you have to keep it."

"I will, Father."

"Blood, boy. A promise like this demands blood."

"No, Father, please."

"Don't cry, damn you."

"I'm not crying."

"I never cried, boy. Not once in my life."

"I'm not crying, Father."

"Never let me see you cry. Let me have your arm."

"Will it hurt, Father?"

"Has it hurt before?"

"Yes."

"And did the pain go away?"

"Yes, Father."

"Just as it will this time."

The voices whispered through the memories locked in Ris's mind as he sat in the quietness of the room. He kept his eyes closed tightly, at home in the darkness. It had been years since he had actually heard his father's voice, had experienced the chill that knotted up his stomach every time he had been forced to make the promise. His arms still showed the scars of the wounds that had been inflicted. It was true that the pain did go away, and it was true that he could never actually remember it even the next day. There had been matching scars on his father's arms. They had sat cross-legged on the floor of this very room, even as he was now, with only the knife and the lighted candle between them. Even old Kettwig had never

been invited to their ceremony, never been asked to join
their promise. It had belonged to his father and him.
Their secret. Their promise.

Hesitantly he reached out a hand without opening his
eyes, taking up the SIG-Sauer P-226 from its place on the
stone floor. The tactile contact with the cold, heavy pistol reminded him of the last promise. His hands had been
covered with blood. He had been covered with blood.
Had tasted it on his lips.

He didn't understand the implications of everything his
father had told him, nor of what Kettwig seemed to stay
constantly involved in. But he knew he was an important person. His father had told him that his whole life.
Even the other old men Kettwig sometimes introduced
him to seemed to be impressed with his abilities.

Ris knew how to act when he met people like that, just
as he knew how to give the speeches Kettwig wrote for
him from time to time to present to the officers. His father had drilled him to perfection in those abilities just as
he had made sure Ris knew how to handle himself with
gun, knife and fist.

Raising the pistol, Ris kept his eyes shut. He felt the
coolness of the muzzle push into his temple. For a moment he considered pulling the trigger. For seven years he
had lived without his father, continuing the training that
had become part of his life. He taught what he knew to
hand-picked units, growing into an uneasy manhood as
he saw people learn to use what he had given to them. He
took training from others, learning the different martial
arts of the Orientals his father had never allowed, touching the different thought processes of the teachers he had
hired to train him until he learned enough to kill them
and send whatever secrets they had learned of the underground complex to the grave with them. None of them

had ever lasted longer than two years at the most. His father had created the perfect pupil, a being who burned with the need to learn quickly and just as quickly faulted the teacher once everything had been taught.

For the seven years his father had been dead, Ris had spent most of them empty and alone. Until he rediscovered Helene when the girl had followed the trail that reached back to the complex.

What would his father think of him if he pulled the trigger?

"Coward." The word whipped out of the nowhereness of the dark bedroom. There was no mistaking the voice.

Ris blinked his eyes open. "Father?" His voice sounded strange in his ears, and he knew he had never physically heard the other voice. It had been a gust of memory sailing across his subconscious.

A light tap sounded at the door.

Uncoiling, Ris stood and padded barefoot to the door, still holding the SIG-Sauer at his side. An aide rolled a service tray into the room when he opened the door. He knew Kettwig had sent the food up and didn't bother to speak to the aide. Once the table leaves were locked into place, the man left, executing a snappy salute.

Ris ignored the silver-covered dishes and climbed onto the massive bed. Food was the farthest thing from his mind. Didn't Kettwig know Helene was missing? Didn't the man know how much she meant to him? How she made him feel?

He tucked the pistol under his pillow and turned his mind loose, dropping into troubled dreams where he kept searching for Helene behind locked doors and kept finding his father instead.

"A final pact," his father told him in the dream when Ris could no longer escape.

"No." Ris felt panic rise in him in the dream. The candle burned brightly between them. He felt the weight of the gun pressed into his hands.

His father's voice was hoarse and harsh. "Yes, boy. A final pact between us."

"No."

"A promise, boy."

"No, Father."

"Take the gun, boy. Hold it here, under my chin. Tightly, damn it. Tighter, boy. You don't want to miss."

"No blood, no blood."

"Put your finger on the trigger with mine."

"Please . . ."

"You've got to be strong."

"I will, Father."

"Promise me you'll do what we have talked about."

"I promise."

"Kettwig will help you. I've instructed him."

"I know."

"I love you, boy."

"I love you, Father."

"Pull the trigger."

The remembered explosion rocked Ris into a deeper blackness where the dreams and memories couldn't get at him, submerged him in nothingness where he felt safe.

9

From his airborne position, Bolan watched the line of black limousines thread through the Washington streets. The helicopter he rode in swept back and forth across the vehicles and the surrounding buildings as the pilot, Jack Grimaldi, shadowed the motorcade's movements.

So far everything had gone exactly as planned. The Russian jet had landed at the airport seven minutes ahead of schedule, and the security teams waited until the proper time before leaving the airfield. The Russian guards had understood the reason for waiting and seemed to be at ease with the delay.

Shifting in the seat, Bolan brought his binoculars to his eyes again, scanning the horizon, then focusing on the streets below. Static squeaked in his ear as the security teams involved in the transportation effort ticked off their numbers. Gorbachev was in the fourth car back. The second car was manned entirely by an American security team and flew the diplomatic flags from the fenders. Hopefully, if any action was taken on the streets, the attackers would concentrate their efforts on it.

"How does it look?" Grimaldi asked over the intercom.

Bolan consulted his watch. It was just after ten o'clock. "Timewise we're doing fine. The problem is we can't be sure how far our security has been penetrated. For all we know, even our little cadre has become suspect."

"Trust the other guy only as long as you can see him."

Bolan nodded. "Something like that. And Mike Belasko has got a lot of markers against him. The tension this morning was so thick you could cut it with a knife."

Grimaldi made a slight adjustment on the control stick, and Bolan felt the helicopter yaw to the left.

"They're playing you as the odd man out?"

"Yeah. Normally it's the role I enjoy most when dealing with the government, but now it puts me out of reach of the operation's nerve center. Anything I can do is going to be pure reaction."

"How much do the Russians know?"

"Everything. The President insisted on it. So did Hal."

"And they still want the meeting?"

"Hell, Jack, they don't have a choice. Russia has been making a lot of overtures with its *glasnost*. Gorbachev is having to back members of his own cabinet to make this meet possible. A lot of them are saying the United States can't control the factions within its own government. Others are saying the situation has been manufactured so that no blame can be placed on the United States if something happens to Gorbachev."

"Has Aaron had any luck identifying that tattoo?"

Bolan shook his head. "Not yet. There's nothing in our files at all that relate to terrorist activity or a mercenary group. There have been some oblique references to it over the years in police files when guys have been arrested, but even those are doubtful because there are no pictures. So maybe the tattoo has a history that has touched the authorities before and maybe it hasn't."

"It doesn't seem likely that something this big would choose now to check into reality."

"No. There's a purpose for this, Jack. We just haven't found it yet." Bolan blinked his eyes, feeling them burn as he forced himself to stay awake. There had been no time for sleep when he had returned to Stony Man after everything had been straightened out with the Fairfax PD. Hal Brognola was concerned over the sanctity of the security operation and with good reason. Publicity had been impossible to avoid. Bolan's recent activities with the Witness hits and with Dwight Hooker had pushed the Belasko name up into the glitz of the morning papers. The *Washington Post* had run front-page space on "Belasko," using the information provided in the file Bolan and Kurtzman had engineered. His presence, though requested from the Man, had become something of a liability on the project.

Bolan adjusted the harness webbing him into the seat of the helicopter. He'd removed his jacket when he climbed in, and unstrapped his weapons belt. The black turtleneck he wore felt scratchy against his neck. A modified Galil married to an M-203 grenade launcher occupied space at his feet. With Grimaldi at the controls of the helicopter, he felt sure he could react with speed and thunder if it was required. If anything came at them from the air, a contingent of Navy top gun pilots were waiting only minutes away. As well, the helicopter Grimaldi piloted wasn't totally defenseless. Chain guns and a four-pod rocket launcher were hidden from the eye by false hulls.

The consequences of a successful assassination of either the U.S. President or the Soviet leader had paraded through Bolan's mind the whole morning. No matter which country lost the head of its government, the feeling of camaraderie that had begun to develop between the United States and Russia during the past few years would cease to exist.

There *would* be an attack. Bolan was sure of it. He could only hope that the security teams would be able to keep whoever was stalking the leaders off balance, even if they didn't believe in the threat as strongly as Bolan did.

BOLAN STOOD in the glass elevator, forcing himself to relax. He looked down through the twelve-floor atrium as the elevator dropped almost fast enough to make him weightless. For a moment it seemed as if the cage would plunge into the pool of water on the bottom floor, then all motion ceased and the doors whispered open.

The main hotel lobby was packed with people taking a break from convention proceedings, and Bolan made his way through the crowd with a polite smile and a firm hand.

He recognized one member of the Justice Department's security team standing near the entrance and nodded slightly to let the man know nothing was happening on the upper floors. The ruse to switch Gorbachev and his party from Blair-Lee house on Pennsylvania Avenue had been an early idea of his, and they had stuck with it. Now, lodged at one of the finer hotels in the Washington, D.C., area, the Russians were logged as a group of Hollywood moguls looking for a place to shoot a new movie. The Russian president had seemed to enjoy the disguise despite the reason for the subterfuge.

Bolan sauntered to a bank of pay phones and placed a long-distance call to Johnny Tallin in New York. He'd left a message earlier for the Mafia security chief to be there when he called back. That had been a little over two hours ago, after the Russians had been installed in the top floor of the hotel. The penthouse suite was empty except for Russian and American security teams. Bolan had designed it as a deadly no-man's-land in case the helicopter attack that had been used to hit Kirby Howell was used again.

The warrior checked his watch: 1:05. A security meeting had been set up for two. According to Gorbachev's agenda, dinner at the White House was planned for this evening. Bolan wasn't looking forward to it.

The phone rang in his ear twice before Tallin picked it up.

"Johnny?"

"Yeah."

"What have you got on those dead guys?"

Tallin sighed tiredly, and Bolan guessed the younger man hadn't made it back to bed, either. "Let's just say that if everything I came up with turned to piss, you wouldn't have enough to float a toothpick."

"Let me hear what you have. Maybe it'll fit in with some of the things I've turned up."

Paper rustled. "Okay. I got names on all three guys from a cop contact we keep on the payroll."

Bolan pushed away the momentary feeling of anger. He had known when he requisitioned Tallin that he was going to learn more than just details about the dead man. As long as there were crooks, there were going to be crooked cops. Once he was through with current business, he intended to look into Patrizio Madrano's affairs himself. Tap into a little intel on the streets Executioner-style until something gave. Leo and Hal could pick up the pieces.

"Does it matter which one was which?"

"No."

"James Harvey was an electrician licensed through the state of New York and had lived there for the past eight years. Robert McGinty was an accountant working for the IRS in a New York City branch. Wayne Hermann was a security guard working for Spraggue Industries in Fairfax, Virginia."

"You're sure about the last guy?" Bolan asked.

"Yeah. Mr. Madrano has a Family guy down in D.C. who owes him a favor. He checked it out at Mr. Madrano's request."

"Hermann was currently employed by Spraggue Industries?"

"Yes."

"In what capacity?"

"Just a guard, I guess. The guy didn't check into it too closely. You sound like this is something hot."

"Maybe," Bolan said, making sure none of the enthusiasm he felt made its way into the icy voice he was using. "Where did Hermann live?"

"In an apartment complex in Fairfax."

"You got a name on the complex?"

Tallin gave it and Bolan wasn't surprised to learn it was the same as Dwight Hooker's.

Bolan said, "Why would a guy from Virginia be there with two guys from New York?"

Apparently Tallin didn't take the question as rhetoric and figured he needed to answer. "I'm assuming he was heading up the operation on this end."

"Why?"

"This guy was carrying the bankroll, Omega. In a money belt around his waist."

"What did the Spraggue Industries people say about Hermann's death?"

"They don't know he's dead yet. I'm setting up an 'accident' so the bodies can be discovered later. The guy in D.C. acted as if he was a loan officer at a bank and Hermann had applied for a loan on a new car. He told me he had the impression the secretary he talked to didn't believe him about the loan. He couldn't figure it. Borrowing money is the American way."

"Did you get a social security number on these guys?" Bolan took a pad and pen from inside his jacket and wrote them down as Tallin read them off.

"I'm going to keep checking on a few other things on this end," Tallin said, "but first I'm going to catch up on a few winks."

"Catch a few for me," Bolan said, and hung up. He tapped the pen on the pad thoughtfully. Finally he had a common denominator: Spraggue Industries. But where did that leave him? He wasn't sure. At least now he had a rock to turn over to see what squirmed out. He dialed an exchange that was redirected to Stony Man without being traceable.

"Kurtzman," the Bear's voice rumbled.

"Striker," Bolan said.

"How's it going?"

"So far, so good," Bolan said as he leaned into the telephone to allow a man in a three-piece suit wearing a party hat to pass. "I think I've got something for you to sink your teeth into this time."

"It will definitely be a change of pace, Striker. I'm beginning to feel like a researcher for *People* magazine with the amount of bios I've been pulling and like a researcher for *National Enquirer* with the way I've been searching for that damn tattoo of yours. I've even had guys checking out tattoos the bikers are into out in

Oklahoma. I haven't been able to turn up anything like it.''

"You'll still be doing profiles, but now we're looking for more specific things."

"Gimme."

Bolan read off the social security numbers Tallin had collected, then added the names.

"I can have these for you in a few minutes, Striker."

"Take some time with it," Bolan said. "And pay particular attention to Wayne Hermann's file."

"Any special reason?"

"Just a feeling," Bolan replied, "plus the fact that the guy worked as a security guard for Spraggue Industries."

The Bear turned thoughtful. "The same place where Hooker moonlighted."

"Right."

"Do you think we have something here?"

"Yeah. Wayne Hermann headed up the hit team that tried to take me out in New York." Bolan could hear Kurtzman tapping computer keys in the background.

"Spraggue Industries," Kurtzman mumbled more to himself than to Bolan. "Specializing in imports and exports. Got an impressive Dun and Bradstreet listing, Striker."

"Who owns it?"

More tapping sounded in Bolan's ear. "Ah." Kurtzman sounded intrigued. "There I'm running into a snag, Striker."

"No names jump out at you immediately?"

"Not that. I've got plenty of names, but this looks suspiciously like a runaround. Yeah, yeah. Uh-huh. It's definitely more complicated than a normal tax evasion dodge. I think you've struck pay dirt, guy, but it's going to be a while before I can let you know anything definite."

"Just stay with it, Aaron."

"You got it. Oh, *this* is interesting."

Bolan waited, watching the convention people constantly shifting into different little groups centering around the vast panorama of plants, statues and fountains in the main lobby.

"Spraggue Industries apparently has a subsidiary in Cairo. But it doesn't have a listing for the owners or corporate people, either. Yeah. This is going to take a while, Striker."

"Get back to me when you can."

"Right."

Bolan broke the connection as he digested the new information. Maybe it wouldn't seem significant to Brognola or the other security teams, but Cairo was only a few heartbeats from Libya. Would the trail eventually end there? Khaddafi had made a lot of threats about terrorists in the United States. Was that promise coming to fruition? In some ways the scenario fit. The teams were definitely trained in military maneuvers, and damn well equipped.

A blond woman held the elevator doors open for him, and he smiled his thanks, moving over so that the guy behind him could get in, too. Bolan reached out and tapped the button for the twelfth floor, watching as she selected the seventh for herself.

Warning bells tripped in his mind when he noticed that the man who had entered the car at the last minute didn't punch a button. As he studied the man's reflection in the glass walls of the elevator, Bolan tried to place him. The guy was lean, no older than mid-twenties, and had short brown hair. The blue suit was pressed and tailored, not off the rack. The buttons on the jacket were moved over enough to allow the jacket to conceal a shoulder rigging. Then Bolan placed him as a member of one of the security teams fielded by the NSA.

The woman walked to the glass wall of the elevator overlooking the fountain area, an embarrassed smile on her face. "These things always make me dizzy," she said, "but I'm just not athletic enough to take the stairs."

A sudden explosion ripped through the building and shook the elevator shaft. Bolan realized at once that it had come from the upper stories. He reached for the Desert Eagle just as the man standing next to the control box hit the Stop button. Then the guy slipped his hand under his jacket and came away with a snub-nosed .38.

The woman screamed and whirled away from the glass wall just as the window shattered and the cage was filled with bullets. Bolan dived for the guy, gripping him in a stranglehold by the tie and propelling him toward the broken glass wall of the elevator. He used the weight of the heavy .44 to knock the revolver away, then pitched the man out of the cage. The fountain area was clear of any pedestrians and was four stories down. The Executioner dropped to a prone position, the .44 extended in front of him.

Scanning the floors on the opposite side of the atrium, Bolan found the shooter one flight down, partially hidden behind a row of potted plants that dangled over the railing. The Executioner squeezed off two shots as the man was bringing his rifle to his shoulder. The flat-nose silhouette slugs impacted in the shooter's upper right chest, spinning him around and sending the rifle flying. The third round from the big Magnum took off the top of the assassin's skull as the man tried to stand up.

The woman was crying hysterically and cringed from Bolan as he tried to reassure her. He switched on the elevator's power again and pulled the microsized walkie-talkie from his belt. "Hal," he called over the command channel that linked him with Brognola.

"Striker? Where the hell are you?"

"Coming your way," Bolan said. Pale cracklings tunneled through the walkie-talkie speaker, slightly louder than the autofire the Executioner could pick up with his own hearing. The elevator stopped at the seventh floor, and he helped the woman from the car after making sure none of the bullets had touched her. Then he punched the button for the eleventh floor, knowing whatever forces were engaged with the security teams upstairs would be covering the elevators if at all possible. "How many players have you counted on their side?"

"I don't know. Hell, half of their guys used to be our guys before the explosion."

Bolan swore. He was sure the figures Brognola had named were exaggerated, but how far did the organization reach into their ranks? There was no way to tell at the present. "Where are you, Hal?"

"With Gorbachev."

"Has he been hurt?"

"Not yet. But every man in this room is wondering who's on his side and who isn't. Bowen dropped a Russian agent in the hallway who had a bead on me."

"Look for me," Bolan said as he put the walkie-talkie away. He drew the Beretta with his left hand and slipped the safety off. When the elevator cleared the tenth floor, he moved to one side of the entrance and waited for the doors to open.

The corridor was filled with curious and panicked people, but no one carrying weapons. Bolan moved out in an easy run, holding the Desert Eagle across his chest to move into instant target acquisition, keeping the 93-R to guard his back.

He swung the door open on the stairwell, expecting to come under fire. Nothing. He raced up the steps only to find that the doors opening onto the restricted eleventh floor were locked. He fired two rounds from the .44 into the lock, and sparks flashed from the brass-colored metal. He loaded a fresh clip into the Desert Eagle and kicked the door open.

Acrid smoke, cut with some kind of gas that irritated the sinus membranes and throat, spilled from the hallway. Rapid poppings of 5.56 mm ammunition punctured the roiling artificial fog.

A man wearing a gas mask stepped forward and took shape against the smoke.

Bolan leveled the .44 as the man raised his M-16. A double onslaught of 240-grain skullbusters ripped through the gas mask and exploded out the back of the man's head. Before the man's body hit the carpeted floor, another goggled face materialized in the thick smoke above a blossoming flower of muzzle-flashes.

Throwing himself forward, Bolan fired as he fell, watching in grim satisfaction when the goggled face jerked back into the darkness of the smoke as if seized by an invisible giant hand.

There were more bodies in the hallway. Some were wearing gas masks, and some he was able to recognize from the airport and the security briefing earlier in the morning. Russian and American blood stained the expensive carpet, and the man in Bolan mourned the loss of comrades in arms while the soldier in him kept his feet moving, pursuing the hellground.

Bolan paused at the corner of the hallway, pulling on a gas mask that he'd taken from one of the bodies. His eyes watered from the earlier exposure to the gas, blurring his vision. He breathed gently, trying to relax his pain-racked lungs. A fit of coughing almost doubled him over, but he forced himself to press forward.

He seized an abandoned M-16 on his way to the next wing and checked its magazine just before he checked the hallway. The weapon was almost fully charged. Two gas-masked figures waited for him across the hall from Gorbachev's suite.

The Russian president's rooms were spacious, rivaling the penthouse in its luxuries. The door to the suite now hung haphazardly from one hinge, and a body lay spilled halfway into the hall.

Bolan jerked his walkie-talkie free. "Hal?"

"Yeah."

"How are you doing?"

"We're holding up, Striker. The backup teams are on their way."

"Get the president ready. I've got two guys waiting out here. I'm going to take them out, then we've got an eleven-story hike down to ground level. I don't want to chance the elevators."

"Agreed."

The warrior put the walkie-talkie away and swung into the hallway, the M-16 at waist-level. The two guys tried to get out of the line of fire, but a blistering figure eight punched them against the wall behind them.

Bolan threw down the empty weapon and drew the Desert Eagle. He flicked on the walkie-talkie. "It's me, Hal. I'm coming through." He pushed the broken door to one side and stood covering the exit. Nothing moved in the hallway, and the smoke seemed to be gradually dissipating through the hotel's ventilation system.

Brognola led the way out, fisting a .38 long-barreled Colt revolver. The head Fed took up a position just outside the door and waved the remainder of the security team out of the suite. Gorbachev followed last, almost covered in the human armor of his security people.

"Are you all right, sir?" Bolan asked as the Russian president drew even with him.

"Yes, thank you," he replied in his thick accent.

Bolan watched the man's eyes widen at the carnage left behind by the lifting smoke. He took off the gas mask so that Gorbachev could see his face. "Please don't stop. We need to get you out of this building as soon as possible."

"So many are dead."

"Yes, sir. But we have to leave."

"Yes, of course."

"Belasko."

Bolan turned to face Alexi Kuryakin, Gorbachev's chief of security. The man was squat and swarthy, powerfully built, deadly in a miniature sort of way like the Uzi he held across his broad chest.

"Where do we go from here?"

"Down," Bolan replied, "just as soon as we figure out how many of us are left."

The Russian nodded and snapped his fingers at one of his men. A compact radio was produced, and he barked orders into it. Different voices began answering.

Bolan glanced around and found the heads of the NSA teams and Greg Bowen, the section chief for the CIA force. "Call your guys," he ordered, "and get me some status reports quick." He saw resentment flare briefly in Bowen's eyes and felt like an outsider. Yeah. Hell, he was an outsider here despite the presidential invitation. The argument he had presented at the meeting this morning had been ignored by the men he was surrounded by. Now evidence of what he had been saying was lying dead at their feet.

Once the different security heads had their figures, Bolan broke into the channel, his words translated for the Russian contingent.

"We're bringing the president down and out," the Executioner said. "Keep everyone away from the stairwell on the south side. That's the one we'll be using. Don't let anyone use those doors. We're going to be securing them as we go. We'll coordinate the movements on this frequency. I want all local law-enforcement people kept away from us. I want no contact with anyone outside of our group. And you people who are presently separated from us had better stay away, as well."

The Russian translator finished a heartbeat after he did.

Bolan turned to Greg Bowen. "You did recon work for the Marines for a few years?"

Bowen nodded.

"Good. You're going to be working point with me."

Bowen nodded again and recovered an M-16 from the floor, stripping a nearby body of extra cartridges. Bolan moved across the hallway and did the same.

"Hal, I want you and Kuryakin on the president, and move only when I say." He snapped a fresh clip into the assault rifle.

"When we clear the area, Hal," Bolan continued, "I want Justice to do a thorough mop-up here. I want to know every man's personal history since the day he was born, and I want to know where those weapons came from."

Ice Wolf

"You'll have it," Brognola promised.

Bolan took his friend's hand and shook it. "Good luck, Hal."

"Yeah. Good luck to both of us."

10

For a moment Kettwig stared down at the sleeping man in silence and remembered the boy he had helped raise. Reluctantly he reached out to shake the man's shoulder, wishing he could let Ris sleep. But he couldn't. His presence was demanded by some of the people who helped support the movement and were wanting reassurance that everything was going as planned.

Even as his fingers touched the younger man's flesh, Ris became a blur of motion. Before Kettwig had the chance to blink, he found himself staring down the barrel of a SIG-Sauer.

"What are you doing here?" Ris asked as he lowered his weapons.

"We have an audience within the next hour," Kettwig explained as he limped toward the closet built into the wall. "You need to speak to some people, to give them reassurances. Some things have happened while you slept that will have to be explained."

"What things?"

Kettwig glanced over his shoulder, noting that Ris had sat up. The young man looked strained, tired. The general had noticed that the dinner he had sent Ris hadn't been touched. One of the first things that would be attended to before the meeting would be a proper breakfast. "The attempt on the Russian president failed."

"As it was supposed to."

"True, but the attack didn't take out as many of the Russian security team as we had planned. Nor was the decision made for the Russians to leave Washington."

"They are staying for the meetings?"

"Yes." Kettwig watched in satisfaction as Ris took in the news and started mulling over the variables and possibilities.

"We still have our links to the Star Wars program and its Russian equivalent?"

"Yes. Our satellite will be positioned perfectly by tomorrow morning to coincide with the White House greeting. I'm told we can effectively jam both systems at the same time."

Ris pushed himself off the bed. "Who's getting nervous?" Ris asked.

"I didn't say anyone was getting nervous," Kettwig replied as he pulled a black suit from the closet. "But a meeting has been called."

"Who will be there?"

"The representatives from Russia, Libya and East Germany. Maybe a few of the others."

"And what will they want to hear?"

"That everything is going according to plan."

"We are setting out to destroy a world," he said. "What kind of tolerances do they believe such an endeavor should be allowed?"

Kettwig never ceased to be amazed at the character changes Ris was capable of. How many different personalities had his father psychologically embedded into the boy's psyche as he was growing up? Politician, warrior, child, they were all there in full doses, and Ris succeeded in controlling them when he needed to, presenting each face in turn just as he had been trained to. It was this ability that would help elevate him in stature above the survivors of the war they were determined to bring about—that and the army that was ready to follow him. Kettwig felt sure as he watched the younger man dress and saw the fire glinting in the mad blue eyes that a new Germany would rise from the ashes of the old just as Ris's father had promised. Already Ris had persuaded powerful men to join forces with him.

Total chaos would rule the globe for a while, Kettwig knew, and a dark part of him considered the conquest hungrily. Once the final split was made between the United States and Russia, once the final straw of suspicion and distrust was added to the back of detente, then it would be time to trigger the satellite jamming system and show both countries that the other had started a nuclear attack. There would be instant retaliation.

It would take years for the balance of world power to shift again, and Kettwig knew he wouldn't live to see it. But he could position people around Ris, could protect their future by careful selection of allies as the struggle took place. There would be a new Germany, one not divided by a damn wall, where the German people could live in pride again. It was what he and Ris's father had spent most of their lives planning.

"I've got a few notes together in my office," Kettwig said. "We'll have something to eat and we'll talk with the representatives. We only need their cooperation a little while longer, then it will be survival of the fittest."

"What about our contacts in America?" Ris asked as he shrugged into a shoulder holster. "Our agents in the hierarchy of the Ku Klux Klan and the Aryan Guard? Are they in need of reassuring as well?"

Kettwig smiled in spite of the pain gnawing at his leg. "They are of German blood, however thinned. They are waiting, biding their time like jackals until the lion is brought down. They will be there when we need them."

Ris's face softened. "Has there been any word of Helene?"

Kettwig bit his tongue, feeling the familiar anger flame to life within him, but he knew better than to say anything about the way he felt.

"I don't want her harmed," Ris said. "I want you to make sure the men understand that."

"I know."

Ris pulled on the matching jacket and walked from the room without a backward glance.

Kettwig limped to the door and started to shut it, taking the time for a last glance at the bedroom. Nothing had been changed in the room from the time Ris's father had lived in it. Maps of old Prussia still adorned the walls. How did Ris feel about occupying the room? Could he feel the burning force that had driven his father, the desire for vengeance?

Kettwig could.

He had lived those feelings with the man and marveled at all he had been able to put together.

But the thing that drove Ris was somehow more darkly evil than just a need for revenge. His father had shaped, bent, broken and reshaped a tool that would change the face of the world. If it could cope with the internal forces that drove it.

Kettwig quietly closed the door and limped after Ris's broad back, wondering what would happen to those people around Ris when the floodgates holding back the lessons of his father proved to be more than he could stand.

HAL BROGNOLA STOOD in the center of the blood-stained hallway and rubbed his eyes with the palms of his hands. Teams of Justice investigators moved throughout the wreckage of the floor, taking samples of everything.

He watched Greg Bowen dodge out of the way of a team of medics carrying a body bag to the gaping hole that housed the elevator. The CIA section chief carried two Styrofoam cups of coffee.

"You like it black?" Bowen asked as he handed Brognola one of the cups.

"Yeah, thanks."

"How's it going?" Bowen asked.

"Slow. It'll be days before they get this sorted out."

"Got any prelims?"

"The medics have carried out twenty-three bodies so far."

"How many of them are ours?"

Brognola stepped out of the way of a coverall-clad guy digging bullets out of the wall behind him. "It's hard to tell with the way things went down here today. By the way, I didn't get the chance to thank you for saving my life earlier."

An easy grin split the CIA man's face. "Purely response of early development at the Agency. A result of believing that whenever something bad goes down around you and you're standing shoulder to shoulder with a Russian, watch the Russian."

"Maybe there were too many of your guys trained that way," Brognola said dryly. "The death rate on the Russians is running almost three to one higher than ours."

"Or maybe more of the Russian security team was infiltrated than any of our guys. Gorbachev's policies have divided Russia in a lot of ways. Most of the populace is behind his thinking, but a lot of the politicians and soldiers cut their teeth on Lenin's teachings and want to keep it that way."

"Yeah, I know, but it puts the United States in a hell of a spot. The news services have already picked this up, and the speculations are going crazy."

"The truth isn't so sane, either, Hal. You and I both know the kind of planning that would have to go into an operation like this. And the agents we had that turned— my God, some of those men have been around for years."

Brognola sipped the coffee. "Yeah, but the same prejudices you've labeled the Russians with easily applies to us, as well. I know a lot of guys in high places who aren't thrilled with the idea of the U.S. doing anything more with Russia than negotiating a way to get rid of some of the nuclear arms buildup. They still want wars between us over Third World countries. You'll find hawks on both sides of the iron curtain, Greg."

"I know. Hell, we both live it every day."

Brognola nodded.

"Where's Belasko?" Bowen asked.

Brognola checked the younger man's face for any sign of underlying emotion. He had noted the friction between the CIA section chief and Bolan during the evacuation of the hotel. "Following up on some new information he turned up."

"Anything interesting?"

"He thinks so."

"What?"

Brognola looked Bowen in the eye and lied through his teeth. "I haven't been briefed yet." Bolan would need as much time as he could get to pursue the almost intangible trail he had uncovered without any of the other agencies muddying the water.

"I thought Belasko was working through your department."

"He is, but he's also working on his own. He's had his own contacts working on this thing since he signed on."

"And they turned up something we haven't been able to?" Bowen seemed skeptical.

"Belasko is a specialist in things like this. I told you that earlier. Which is why the President gave him a free rein when it came to this operation. He's damn good at what he does."

"I still have problems believing there could be a guy like this who I haven't heard of."

A man down the hall called to Brognola, holding one of the confiscated M-16s above his head as he kneeled before a portable scrambler phone.

The big Fed walked away from Bowen, wishing there was some way to resolve the distrust the younger man felt for Bolan. But he couldn't blame the guy. After the fiasco at the hotel, who the hell could you trust?

"What have you got, Henderson?" Brognola asked as he took the assault rifle.

Henderson's eyes were narrowed in disgust. "I traced those weapons, sir, and you're not going to like it one damn bit."

A sinking feeling swirled in the big Fed's stomach. He had assumed the American weapons had been purchased on the black market, but the look in the Justice investigator's eyes told a different story. "Let's have it."

"WHO IS THIS MAN?" Ris tapped the photograph with a forefinger. It was an almost full-face shot of the same man in the dozen other pictures he had scanned through.

Kettwig sat on the other side of the desk in his office. They had met there because it was where the older man had assembled everything they had received so far and because Ris felt more comfortable there than in his own office. He smelled the minty aroma of the schnapps as Kettwig poured himself another glass.

"His name is Michael Belasko," Kettwig said. "From what we have been able to find out about him, the man is some kind of free-lance security consultant who has the uncanny ability to drop off the face of the world for months at a time."

"How did he become involved with protecting the Russians?" Ris studied the face with interest. There was a kinship there, lying just under the surface of the craggy features. Belasko had been marked by close-up views of the blitzkrieg even as Ris's father had marked him.

"The American President requested he be on hand for the meeting." Kettwig sipped the schnapps. "So far Belasko has preempted a strike against one of the Witness Protection people we've been liquidating in an attempt to divide the attention of the Washington, D.C., law-enforcement agencies. And he terminated a three-man team we had watching one of the Mafia dons who hired our assassination team. He uncovered the man we had planted on the Washington police force and left the agent no choice but to take his own life. He was also the man who led the Russian leader to safety after the hotel assassination attempt."

"This man is no simple security consultant," Ris concluded as he laid the photograph on Kettwig's desk with the others.

"No. But he is the man you'll have to go through in order to complete the assassinations."

"It will be this man's mistake to get in my way." Ris pushed himself up out of the swivel chair in front of the desk, wishing there was a window in the office so that he could look out over the desert. He loved it most at night, when the sun was beginning to fall and life truly began to move across the shifting sands. He and Kettwig had completed their short talk with their constituents more than an hour ago, when he had announced he would be seeing to the deaths of the American and Soviet leaders himself. It had been a contingency on the original plan he and Kettwig had advanced to them, but one that would bring them a larger following after the war that would surely follow.

So now, following the plan his father had given birth to long before he had a son, Ris would be stepping into the position of power his father had coveted so fiercely. Maybe, if it hadn't been for the promise he had given his father, he would have walked away from it all at this point. Now that the time was here, there seemed to be nothing grand at all about it. He was surprised that the prospect of success left him feeling so empty. Perhaps, had his father remained alive, there would be some thrill in the undertaking. But, for now, there was only the mechanics of the assassinations to double-check. There would be those fleeting moments of pleasure when he stroked the trigger of the assassination weapon and sent death winging into the two world leaders. But that wouldn't last long. It never did.

BOLAN GAVE UP trying to follow the progression of documents Kurtzman was showing him. It was making his head hurt.

Kurtzman looked over his shoulder with an apologetic look on his face. "I know this is pretty dry stuff,

Mack, but I wanted you to see what you were facing. The
parent company for Spraggue Industries goes back at
least forty years. Maybe more. They had connections and
holdings in several countries. Whoever has been helming this operation during those years has had a lot of
capital to invest. And still has a lot of bucks to spread
around.''

"Enough to buy off security people in America and the
Soviet Union," Turrin observed.

Bolan shook his head. "There's more to it than that,
Leo," he said, remembering the fanaticism that had
shone from Dwight Hooker's eyes. "Remember the guy
who blew himself up in the arcade?"

"Yeah."

"These guys don't mind sacrificing themselves if it
comes down to it, as long as they can take somebody with
them."

"Like terrorists."

"Or like they were fighting a war," Bolan said. He
readjusted himself on the edge of Kurtzman's desk,
wishing Brognola would hurry up and call in with the report on the hotel hit. They were on the edge of something; he could feel it humming in his bones.

"But why do the Witness hits?" asked Leo Turrin,
who was sitting in on the briefing.

"For effect," Bolan replied. "As a diversion it served
to pull attention away from the main issue we were covering. Yet it failed in one aspect because it let us identify
the fact that the two operations were connected. Of
course whoever set this up hadn't planned on my tag-
ging Wayne Hermann or noticing Hooker plant the bug
on my car in D.C."

"How did you figure the two situations were re-
lated?" Turrin asked.

"Hooker put the tracer on my car before I got involved with you. Which meant the guy was trying to get a fix on me concerning the security for the armament talks. At the time he didn't know I was going to be involved in your end of things. The tattoo made the final connection between the two."

"Hal said they only found a couple of guys with the tattoo at the hotel," Kurtzman said.

Bolan nodded. "And when we get the skinny on those guys and are able to identify them, I'll bet we find out they were connected in some way to Spraggue Industries. I'd guess those guys to be some kind of elite corps that guided the smaller operations."

"All the while the real target has been the Prez and Gorbachev," Kurtzman said.

"Right," Bolan replied.

"Meaning the Witness hits had no real bearing on the mission at all," Turrin concluded.

"Only as a diversionary tactic," Bolan said honestly. He sensed the anger Turrin was keeping locked in, and it fed the flames burning within his own body. "If you hadn't picked up the thread when you did, Leo, we might not have been able to tumble to this as soon as we did."

"That's cold comfort, Mack."

"I know."

Bolan stood and walked behind Kurtzman, studying the information on the screen against the far wall, as if the new position would add a perspective he hadn't used before. "You're sure that Spraggue Industries has a home base in Cairo, Aaron?"

"There were a lot of circles, Mack, like I said earlier, but I'm sure. Everything leads back to Cairo. At least forty years ago a plan was laid down to build a company, Phoenix Enterprises—guess we're not the only ones who rose from the ashes. The people running the company stayed in business long enough to turn a large profit from the war recovery in Egypt, as building contractors and the like. They did a lot of reconstruction on the city and helped draw up plans for a lot more things.''

''An American company?'' Bolan asked.

''All the paperwork was handled in English,'' Kurtzman affirmed, ''but I couldn't find a listing for the founder of the company. It gives his name as William Thomas, but, hell, Sarge, I could turn up hundreds of William Thomases from the 1940s. It would take weeks to research all of them, even if I had a full staff engaged in doing nothing but that.''

''How long did Phoenix Enterprises stay in business?''

''Almost ten years,'' Kurtzman replied as he checked his notes. ''Then they dissolved and moved on. At least superficially.''

''What do you mean?''

''I mean whoever was running this company took the money they made and invested it in several different businesses around the world. And they were smart about it. The businessmen and legal guys I consulted on this were amazed. The paperwork involved in moving this money around would fill a couple of rooms, and most of this was done before computers were invented. If the buying and trading of businesses hadn't slowed down around the 1970s before home computers became prevalent, I don't think I would have been able to get you the information I have so quickly.''

''Why did they slow down?''

''It had been thirty years since the inception of Phoenix Enterprises. These guys were getting old. Maybe they thought they had covered their tracks well enough. And even at that, if I didn't have access to some of the files I can get into through Interpol and other European agencies, I think I could have been thrown off the track.''

"What happened in the 1970s?"

"Phoenix Enterprises, Incorporated took up residence in one of the buildings the old Phoenix Enterprises had built back in the 1940s.''

"Who had the building before them?"

Kurtzman grinned. "That's an interesting point, because, according to the files I've gone through, the building made the trip with a lot of the businesses that were lost over the years. From what I gathered from an Egyptian real estate broker I talked with earlier, the building had been constructed in a proposed business park south of Old Cairo that never made it.''

"And Spraggue Industries is connected with them?"

"Yes. Also the subsidiary company I told you about. But you won't find that information easily.''

"What kind of business ventures has Phoenix Enterprises, Incorporated been involved in?''

"It's a parent company that owns majority interests in several businesses. Travel, import-export, munitions, a little bit of a lot of things.''

"Sounds as if they can get their hands on pretty much what they want and have a way to move it," Turrin said.

"That's the way it is," Kurtzman agreed. The phone rang and he picked it up.

Bolan stared at the picture of the building that housed Phoenix Enterprises, Incorporated in Cairo.

"Hey, Mack," Kurtzman said in an excited voice.

The warrior switched his attention to Kurtzman, watching as the big man tapped the computer keys and the screen changed obediently.

"I got some information on that tattoo." Kurtzman punched a button by the phone and laid the receiver on the desk. "The guy on the line is Joachim Koltzer, a West German contact in the BND I've used as a resource before. He was a German officer in the Second World War."

Bolan digested the information. Kurtzman had said the connections on Spraggue Industries ran back forty years, and here was another bit of the puzzle that reaffirmed that. "Is this man reliable, Aaron?"

Kurtzman met Bolan's gaze. "I'd trust Joachim with my life. I knew him back when I was working for the Company, and we've always been straight with each other."

Bolan nodded.

Kurtzman hit another button by the phone. "Joachim, it's Aaron. I've got company with me, so I put you on the intercom. These are the men who discovered the tattoo, and they're friends of mine."

"There's not much I have to say at this point, my friends, but I do have something to show you. If your friends feel it's interesting enough, I'll meet with them."

Bolan sensed the hesitation in the thin, reedy voice, heard the age in it, as well. He watched as the monitor screen presented the tattoo in its large dimensions. Then, before he could blink, the picture altered, still showing the bird, but this time overlaid by a huge swastika. The swimming wings formed two of the four hooked ends of the emblem, the profiled head another, the askew tail feathers, with only a little stretch of the imagination, made up the fourth.

"And the bird?" Bolan asked, his voice tight.

"A phoenix," Koltzer said. "Deliberately chosen and stylized the way you see it now before the end of the Second World War."

"Where do you want to meet?" Bolan asked, though he already knew the answer.

"Cairo. Where it was scheduled to be reborn."

11

The Cairo sun beat down on the marketplace, glinting off the shiny trinkets offered for sale at many of the stands and shops. Bolan lounged in the welcome shade of a silversmith's waiting for contact with the Company informer Kurtzman had turned up for the operation. Across the cobbled street filled with tourists and bazaar workers, he could see Leo Turrin lingering over a Coke at a soft drink stand. If the little Fed noticed him, he didn't show it.

Mossad had been called on to lend support, and the three agents who had accompanied Bolan on the flight to Cairo had vanished somewhere in the packed aisles. But Bolan knew they would be near. The commanding officer, Benjamin Tsurnick, was a brief acquaintance the Executioner had made during a previous mission.

In Bolan's analytical mind, it made more sense to go into the present situation with the Israelis as backups since American teams were out of the question. Mossad also had more help sequestered inside Egypt than American forces ever had. Which was how a cache of weapons had come to be waiting for him before he set foot on Egyptian soil.

Bolan shifted uneasily, uncoiling from the cramped position. The numbers were already falling on this one. The Soviet leader's White House appearance was set for the next afternoon, Washington time, and that left less than twelve hours to figure out what was going on and find a way to stop it.

Tsurnick had told him he could put together a team of about twenty-five men for the attempt on the Phoenix building, but it would mean pulling some of the agents out of deep cover.

Even twenty-five men might be too small a force to go up against what Bolan expected to be waiting. The people behind Phoenix Enterprises were forty years ahead of them in planning. And one of the biggest businesses Phoenix Enterprises had immediately following the Second World War was an excavation service. Bolan figured he knew what was being excavated, but not why. It had also given him an idea about how to get inside the building and set up the frontal assault Tsurnick would be leading.

The small wireless earplug in Bolan's right ear crackled with static. "Your man is on his way, Mr. Bolan," one of the Israelis said.

Bolan tapped the Morse button on the transceiver in his jacket pocket and signaled an affirmative. He glanced at his watch and decided Tsurnick and the rest of his force would be in place now, with Grimaldi waiting in the wings with a "broken-down" airliner that wouldn't be fixed until they were ready to leave.

Faisal looked exactly like his CIA file picture, though perhaps a little more frayed around the edges where the sun had worn at him. If Bolan hadn't known from the file that the man was only in his forties, he would have guessed him at least ten years older. A perpetual squint shadowed the man's dark Mediterranean features.

As the man passed, Bolan fell into step with him, taking the folded Egyptian newspaper from his back pocket that contained the money Faisal had requested for the information.

"You are the seeker?" Faisal asked quietly as they continued to walk.

"As surely as the Nile flows north," Bolan responded.

"You have the money?"

"If you have the information."

The Arab nodded.

Bolan did a quick sweep of their surroundings, noticing that Leo had fallen in behind them at a discreet distance.

"I have the information," Faisal said, "but as I told your contact earlier, there is not a lot of information on either Phoenix Enterprises or its owners."

"Are you trying to talk your way out of some of this money?"

Faisal looked at him sharply, then flashed a broad grin. "No, I just don't want you to be surprised at the lack of knowledge my files contain. I have a few pictures, one of which cost the life of the photographer."

"What happened?"

"Thomas shot him."

"William Thomas?"

Faisal shook his head. "No. That was the father. Ris Thomas is the son. It was this Thomas who killed the man who took his picture."

"Charges were never pressed over the murder?"

"What murder?" The Arab's smile was wintery. "When the Tourist Police arrived Thomas was gone and the photographer had a gun in his hand instead of a camera. Obviously the man was not of a sound mind and took his own life. Such thinking makes things much neater in Cairo, true?"

"How did you come by the picture?"

"The photographer was able to run a few steps after he was shot. I recovered the camera in an alley and hid it nearby. Before I could return, my son had died, with no one there to mourn him."

Mentally Bolan pushed the scales of trust a little more in favor of the information broker.

"So you see," Faisal continued, "I have no reason to hide anything from you or even to wonder what it is you want with Thomas or why you seek him. Although I know most people don't use my services unless it bodes ill for whomever I research for them."

Bolan took the Egyptian newspaper from his back pocket and traded it for the thickly rolled one Faisal offered. He rolled the rubber bands off and inspected the contents briefly, noting the handful of black-and-white prints and one color Polaroid shot, along with the pages of printed material spliced into the newspaper's pages. It looked accurate to him, judging from some of the business names he picked up while scanning, though smaller than he had hoped. He rolled the paper back up and replaced the rubber bands.

Faisal smiled with more warmth this time. "As an added bonus," the man said, "the Garfield the Cat comic strip in today's paper is very humorous."

At the far end of the narrow street, a motorcycle ridden by two helmeted men edged slowly through the pedestrians, drawing harsh stares from most of the bazaar-goers. Bolan kept an eye on it as his combat antennae flared to sudden life. Why wear the helmets? The heat in the marketplace was oppressive.

"You will find a picture of a girl in there, as well," Faisal said. "I don't know who she is, but I do know that Ris Thomas has spent considerable manpower looking for her. The picture was taken from one of his agents a few days ago by a pickpocket I know who was convinced it would be worth something to me. Only my wish for vengeance for my son's death convinced me to purchase it and follow up the girl's whereabouts. At present, Thomas still doesn't know where she is, but I do.''

"You think she's important?" Bolan asked as he continued to watch the progress of the motorcycle. It was less than fifty yards away now, stalled in pedestrian traffic. He fingered the collar microphone, which was designed to look like another button on his jean jacket.

"Important enough for Thomas to kill several men two days ago.''

"Where is she?" Bolan asked, realizing the girl might be another lever he could use in some fashion to pry loose whatever secrets lay under the stone foundations of Phoenix Enterprises.

"Normally I would charge another fee for the information," Faisal said as he searched Bolan with intensely brown eyes. "A nominal fee, of course. But in you I see something more than I usually see in the Americans I deal with. You are a warrior. Military at one time. I can see that in your bearing, in some of your mannerisms.''

Bolan remained silent. The motorcycle had gotten under way again, and there was an open area only a little farther on that lay directly in front of the Executioner and his informer. Bolan tucked the newspaper more securely under his arm.

As Faisal started to speak, Bolan saw the man on back of the motorcycle reach into his partner's backpack and pull out an Uzi. The engine on the Japanese bike screamed shrilly as the vehicle lunged forward, spewing black smoke. The staccato burst of noise rebounded from the marketplace's high walls, and people scattered in all directions.

Reacting instinctively, Bolan grabbed a handful of Faisal's djellaba and pulled him toward a small stand filled with jewelry. The roar of the Uzi punctuated the movement as bullets clawed through the air where they had stood.

"Move," Bolan ordered as he kept his hold on Faisal and hurried the man across the wooden countertop of the jewelry stand. The smaller man slid headfirst and dropped from sight. Wooden splinters ripped free of the countertop as Bolan threw himself over in a rolling dive. Glass from display cases shattered, and the small pieces showered the Executioner as he moved to the opposite end of the counter to make sure the clerk was all right. She screamed when he touched her and tried to get away. Bolan held her fast. "Stay down!" the warrior shouted in Arabic.

Satisfied that she understood, he peered over the pockmarked counter to see the driver of the motorcycle heeling the bike around in a tight maneuver that almost laid it on its side. Dust kicked up around it in a semicircle, choking the slower pedestrians still trying to get away.

"Mack," Turrin's voice crackled over the earphone.

"I'm okay," Bolan said into the collar microphone.

"These clowns aren't alone," Turrin went on. "I've got three more bike teams in my sights now."

"Stay clear, Leo. These guys can't hold up an attack for long. The Tourist Police will be here any moment."

"Negative on the no-show, Striker. I just aced the driver on one of the motorcycles. His partners have noticed me, but they seem more interested in you."

"Watch your ass, Leo. If we get separated, I'll meet you back at the rendezvous with Jack."

The buzz-saw whine of the motorcycle erupted as it closed in on the jewelry stand. Bolan watched the rear man drop off as the bike roared forward. He tightened his grip on the newspaper Faisal had given him and drew his Desert Eagle. The Uzi barked again as the motorcycle crashed into the stand, splintering the two-by-fours that formed its skeleton and tearing through the thin plywood skin.

Knowing it would take the driver a moment to reach his weapon, Bolan stood suddenly and pumped two 240-grain hollowpoints through the visor of the man with the Uzi. Crimson froth jetted from the front of the helmet as the gunner was blown backward.

The motorcycle driver tried to get to a standing position and draw the weapon concealed under his jacket at the same time. The heavy Magnum in Bolan's fist thundered twice more and punched fist-size holes through the man's chest.

Stepping over the wreckage of the bike and the jewelry stand, Bolan grabbed Faisal by the elbow and helped the man to his feet. He kicked the side door that opened onto an alley and hustled the smaller man out.

The keening of more motorcycle engines cut through the shrill cries and screams that had suddenly flooded the bazaar. Bolan secured the newspaper inside his jean jacket, pulling Faisal behind him. They were heading toward Khan al-Khalili, a route that led deeper into the maze of the bazaar. The Executioner hoped it would render pursuit by the motorcycles impossible. Once his attackers were on foot, too, the odds for survival would improve dramatically.

How the hell had they gotten onto him so quickly? The only answer he could come up with was that someone had been watching for him at the airport. But how could they be sure he would come? The questions pounded at him faster than his feet on the cobbled alleyway.

Bolan cut into another alleyway, keeping the .44 as much out of sight as possible. He scanned the crowd around him for the white uniform of the Tourist Police with its distinctive green armband and blue strip over the left chest.

Bolan pulled Faisal to one side of the alley and said, "You know this bazaar better than I do and these guys aren't after you. Alone, you stand a better chance of getting away."

The Arab nodded, breathing strenuously, his cheeks puffing with the effort.

"Where's the girl?"

Faisal named the hotel. "She is staying with a woman named McKenna."

"Does anyone else know this?"

"Meaning Thomas or his people? No. Otherwise I'm sure she would no longer be there. Thomas can be a very determined man, as I'm sure you've noticed by now."

"Yeah, I've noticed," Bolan said dryly as he recharged the .44 with a fresh clip. He remembered the helicopter attempt on Kirby Howell and the subsequent clashes he had experienced against Thomas's forces. That the men who served the secret masters of Phoenix Enterprises, Incorporated were so willing to die was alarming enough.

The sound of a motorcycle neared and Bolan turned to go. Faisal stopped him with a hand on his arm. "Good luck."

Bolan nodded.

Moving out at a steady pace, the warrior jogged for the other avenue passing through the bazaar. People scattered before him as if sensing that violence pursued him. He pressed the switch on the collar microphone. "Leo."

"Still in one piece, Striker."

"Find your fastest way out of here and take it."

"Mr. Bolan?"

Bolan answered the call, recognizing the voice as belonging to one of the three Mossad agents who had accompanied him and Turrin to the bazaar.

"Captain Tsurnick wants me to inform you that he is en route to your position and will pick you up by the Hotel Hussein if you can get there in the next few minutes."

The information let Bolan know that Tsurnick was carefully monitoring the situation and had even hedged his bets concerning the Executioner by having a second radio frequency available for the Israeli's use only. Bolan admitted to himself that it was probably something he would have done if he was in the man's place.

"Tell him I'll be there," Bolan said as he made a sudden turn and struck off in a new direction.

"Yes, sir."

Bolan dodged around a balding man wearing a Mickey Mouse T-shirt, sidestepping the man's wife and their four children. He knew that by running he was drawing a lot of unwanted attention, but he was also cutting down the time he would be tracked through the bazaar area. There were too many people wandering through the marketplace to hope that no outsiders would be injured. He opened the channel on the collar microphone. "Leo?"

"Hotel Hussein, Striker. I got a copy." Turrin sounded winded.

"Don't be late."

"I wouldn't think of it, Sarge."

At the other end of the small thoroughfare was an area dominated by a handful of fortune-tellers advertising different techniques in English and Egyptian. Remembering the map of the bazaar area he had studied while on the plane, Bolan knew that once he reached the fortune-telling area, he could turn left and the narrow street would lead him directly to Shari Gohar ei-Qait and Hotel Hussein.

Before he reached the first booth, a motorcycle appeared on the street he intended to turn south on. Not daring to fire at the two men on the motorcycle because of the crowds, Bolan fled back the way he had come, hoping to find another, more roundabout way of getting to the rendezvous point.

He sprinted for all he was worth, knowing the motorcycle would lurch after him instantly, remembering the man on back had reached for a radio instead of an Uzi this time.

A new sound joined the keening of the Japanese bike, and Bolan looked up to see a helicopter bearing down on his position. All doubts lingering in his mind as to who it belonged to dissipated with the initial burst of .50-caliber machine gun fire that ripped a nearby neon sign to shreds.

Wheeling quickly while the helicopter tried to maneuver to present the machine gunner with another chance, Bolan locked the Desert Eagle into a double-fisted grip and emptied the clip in concentrated fire, zeroing in on the pilot.

The helicopter leaped skyward in immediate response, though the Executioner doubted any of the bullets had scored. He changed clips as he cut back again, making a circular attempt to get back to the fortune-telling section. Whirling rotors overhead let him know the helicopter hadn't given up.

Bolan paused, listening for the sound of the motorcycle that was searching for him. With the helicopter covering the area, he knew there was slim hope of being able to get away unseen. His only alternative lay in speed. And the guys riding the motorcycle were definitely sitting on a source of it.

Desert Eagle in hand, Bolan crept back through the shops, knowing if someone saw him their reaction would signal his position to the assassins. The narrow street he'd just left was in pandemonium. People raced away in all directions.

The motorcycle coasted slowly down the street, coming back in Bolan's direction. The rear man was obviously in contact with the helicopter crew by radio.

Waiting until the motorcycle was almost even with him on the other side of the street, Bolan exploded from between the shops, sprinting toward the cyclists. His feet left the ground in a full flying kick targeted on the rear assassin even as the driver tried to get the man's attention.

Bolan felt his boot connect with the base of the man's skull as he had intended, the impetus of his body driving all of them into the brief security offered by a nearby shop. He heard the man's neck snap even over the whine of the motorcycle, and for a moment they were hidden from the helicopter.

Without wasting time, Bolan grabbed the handlebars and righted the motorcycle, knowing the chopper would be in position over him in seconds. The driver lurched to his feet, grabbing at Bolan's arms in an effort to detain him. The Executioner put a foot on the guy's chest and pushed him away.

Bolan hit the starter with a thumb as the helicopter swung into view overhead. The motor chain-sawed into sudden life, and he pulled the throttle back as he released the clutch. The front tire reared up suddenly, then he had it under control as .50-caliber spikes sheared into the cobbled street just behind him.

Keeping himself low over the handlebars, Bolan rocketed down the twisting aisles, homing in on the fortune-tellers' booths. He struggled to keep both wheels under him as he made the corner. In the distance he could see the placard advertising the Hotel Hussein.

Bullets from the machine gun overhead kicked up a ribbon of dust just ahead of him. He whipped through it and changed sides of the street, watching pedestrians dodge out of his way.

"Bolan."

The warrior recognized Tsurnick's harsh tones immediately. He had to reach across his body with his left hand to trigger the collar microphone. "Yeah?"

"I have you in sight. My team is in the black limousine directly in front of you at the corner of the hotel. When you make the exchange here, turn east and head toward the car park. We'll take care of the helicopter."

A moment of unease flashed through Bolan. With the motorcycle he had a chance of avoiding the helicopter's machine gunner, provided he stayed within proximity of the city buildings. And the Tourist Police or regular Egyptian Police should be en route already. If he followed Tsurnick's instructions, it was all open space.

At the corner he dragged a foot and headed east, blowing past the black limousine as Tsurnick disembarked from the rear with a long tube.

Reaching for a higher gear, Bolan sped toward the mesh wire fence surrounding the parking area, determined to put as much space between himself and the helicopter as possible. He heard the rotors screaming into place above him. Closing in on the fence with no move left open for him, Bolan clamped down hard on both front and back brakes, feeling the motorcycle skid sickeningly under him.

Kicking free of the machine, Bolan rolled across the pavement as bullets chopped into the motorcycle's body, following it as it tried to run up on the fence.

Bolan came to a rest on his knees, the Desert Eagle already fisted in his right hand. He drew target acquisition on the bubble shield of the helicopter. But suddenly a flame shot out of the helicopter's tail. An orange-and-black explosion ripped the chopper from the sky to land in the center of Shari al-Azhar.

As he put the .44 away, Bolan saw Tsurnick drop the LAW to the ground and climb back into the limo. The driver wheeled around the mass of burning wreckage in the street and came to a rocking halt beside Bolan. The Executioner got in gratefully. Tsurnick sat on the other side of the plush back seat.

"Good shooting," Bolan said as he settled in. The limo accelerated quietly. Inside the air-conditioned interior, Bolan felt as if he had become part of another world.

"We were fortunate there were no Egyptian authorities involved," the Israeli captain said honestly. "Otherwise I would have had to leave you to your own devices."

"Which were damn few."

"Agreed."

"Where's Leo?"

Tsurnick pointed ahead.

"He got out okay?"

"Yes."

"What about your men?"

"All of them," Tsurnick replied. "So far Israel's involvement in this hasn't been compromised."

"Let's hope it stays that way."

Tsurnick nodded. "Let's have a look at what you bought in the bazaar."

Bolan removed the newspaper from under the jean jacket and separated the pages of information. He scanned each page in turn, then handed it to the Israeli.

"There's not much here," Tsurnick said. "You had most of this information from your American sources."

"Yeah, but we didn't have any pictures."

Tsurnick tapped the black-and-whites. "These are the men we're pursuing? The ones behind the attempt on Gorbachev's life?"

"Yeah."

He handed Bolan the Polaroid. "Who's the girl?"

"I don't know," Bolan replied as he studied the picture. She was blond and would have been beautiful if it hadn't been for the butchered hair and the haggard expression on her face. She'd been watching someone, Bolan thought, someone she was definitely afraid of. "But Thomas was willing to kill to get her back."

"No matter. The girl is either dead or Thomas has her back."

"Neither," Bolan said as he tucked the information he had gotten from Faisal back into the paper. "According to my informant, the girl's hiding in a nearby hotel."

Tsurnick removed the picture of Ris Thomas from the paper and went over it again.

Bolan had the image etched in his mind. The harsh planes of Thomas's face, the scar over the eye, the wintry nothingness that lay in the torrid depths of the eyes.

"This man is a killer," Tsurnick commented.

Bolan agreed.

"You can see it in his face just as surely as you can see it in ours," Tsurnick said. "But there's one difference between us and this one. This man recognizes no conscience, no sadness at being what he is."

"Which makes me wonder why he would leave seclusion to pursue the girl."

"Especially at this point in time, when whatever they have planned all these long years is about to come to fruition." Tsurnick took a long cigar from his pocket and lit it.

"You're thinking the same thing I am."

"That the girl could be more important than surface value?"

"Yes."

Tsurnick nodded. "Yes. I think that as well." He thumbed the intercom button and got the driver's attention. "What was the hotel?"

Bolan gave the name to the Israeli and settled back to grab a few moments of welcome respite from the physical side of the pursuit. The few hours of sleep he'd been able to manage aboard the Harrier Grimaldi had flown into Israel had only been enough to whet his appetite. Yeah, the tactician inside him said the girl definitely bore more exploration, but it was his humanity that said she needed to be rescued from whatever trouble she had found herself in. He just hoped he wasn't too late.

12

Helene struggled through the layers of the nightmare into wakefulness, clawing through the images of Ris as he told her again and again that he loved her. She didn't dream of a normal life anymore. That lay somewhere in the past. The schools in Naples where her father's money paid her to keep her out of his way. How long ago had that been? She considered the present month and subtracted. Eight months. How in the name of God had she been able to survive all that time?

"I love you, Helene," Ris's voice seemed to whisper to her. "I love you the way I've never been able to love anyone else in my life."

Blinking her eyes open through the hot tears that suddenly came to her, Helene lay quiet, not wanting to wake Constance McKenna. She fisted her pillow under her head tightly, curling into a small ball on the bed.

Cautiously she looked around the hotel room, wondering if the escape was the dream and not the nightmare. Maybe while she slept the Hilton's walls had become the walls of the underground complex. When she saw the sunlight filtering in through the patio windows of the hotel room, an unfamiliar exuberance about life flashed through her. It was followed immediately by the feelings of guilt for involving the American woman in her problems.

But there had been nowhere else to go, she told herself again. Ris had given her no choice but to accept refuge wherever it was offered. Surprisingly the McKenna woman had asked no questions and had limited herself to taking care of Helene's needs. The woman had summoned a hairstylist to the hotel room and ordered clothes that fit Helene very well. And Helene had to admit it felt good being taken care of again. In school there had always been her friends. They had taken her to their parents' houses sometimes on vacations because they knew Helene had no family to go home to. She never tried to explain that her father was always too busy to bother with her. Later, when she realized he wasn't just another corporate executive trying to set up his next million-dollar deal, she wondered why her father hadn't had her killed to make sure there were no loose ends.

Someone knocked at the door.

Pulling the covers up to her chin, Helene rolled over, expecting to see Constance McKenna in the other bed. Sudden terror overwhelmed her when she found the bed empty.

Someone knocked again.

"Krista?"

A feeling of relief washed over Helene when she recognized the McKenna woman's voice coming from the bathroom.

"Yes?"

"Did I wake you?"

"No."

"Good. Will you be a dear and answer that? I'm trying to put my face on and I don't want anyone to see me like this. It's probably room service. I placed an order about an hour ago."

"Okay."

She walked to the door and peered out the peephole. She saw a man standing in the hallway with his head down, holding an armful of roses.

"It's someone with flowers," Helene called out.

"They must be from Bryan, my ex-husband. He's still convinced we need to get back together, though while we were married he was convinced we needed to be divorced. I don't know how he found me here."

Filled with trepidation, Helene unlocked the door and stepped back. When the man raised his head, she recognized him at once—Eric Konig, whose loyalties lay more with Fritz Kettwig than with Ris. Panicked, Helene threw her weight against the door, trying to lock the man out. "Constance, call the hotel security! Please hurry! They've found me!"

The woman ran from the bathroom to the phone between the two beds and lifted the receiver.

Konig exploded against the door, and Helene found herself stumbling backward. She tried to get to her feet as she saw the man lift a pistol and point it at Constance McKenna.

"No!" Helene screamed as she reached for the gun.

The pistol bounced in Konig's hand and whispered once.

Helene looked back over her shoulder to see the woman's body jerk with the impact and fall over the bed. She hurled herself at Konig, knotting her hands into fists. Konig backhanded her across the mouth, and she tasted blood on her lips as she sprawled on the floor. Helene stared at him, putting venom in her words. "Ris will kill you for this."

Konig smiled coldly. "Perhaps he would, bitch, if he knew. But you won't tell him. You've caused enough trouble in his life, and you've endangered our cause more than enough.'' He holstered the gun.

Helene kicked out at him, screaming. Surely someone would hear her; someone had to hear her.

Konig caught one of her feet and dragged her roughly across the carpet toward the window. Using force and slaps, Konig muscled her to a standing position near the patio door.

Still struggling, Helene brought a knee up into Konig's crotch, earning another slap after the man only succeeded in partially blocking the blow. Her senses swam with the sudden onslaught of violence. One eye had swollen shut and she had difficulty breathing through her broken nose. She heard the lock click back on the balcony doors, then one of them slide open. A warm, light wind blew through her short hair. Konig managed to grip both of her wrists in one hand as he forced her backward, out onto the narrow balcony. Helene whipped her head around, getting a dizzying panoramic view of Cairo, then saw nothing but the ground three stories below when the man bent her double over the railing.

She felt Konig's free hand wrap around her thigh and lift her, edging more of her upper body off the balcony railing. Anger burned her bruised face. Why didn't she just let go and have done with it? There would be nothing more to fear then. No possibilities Ris or anyone else could take her life and freedom away from her again. But she fought to maintain her grip. Her head pulsed with the pressure of hanging upside down. Her arms ached and shook from holding on so tightly.

Then an explosion sounded behind her, and she felt the pressure on her legs lessen. Her hands slid down the white wrought iron with bruising intensity, and she knew gravity was going to finish the job Eric Konig had started.

THE BERETTA FILLED Mack Bolan's hand at the first scream. He held the elevator doors open as Tsurnick hit the Stop button.

He glanced down the empty hallway, realizing most of the hotel guests would be out of their rooms, engaged in whatever business or pleasure had brought them to Cairo. The scream sounded again. Bolan wasn't able to pinpoint the source, but he was fairly certain it was coming from room 312, where Faisal said he would find the girl Ris Thomas was searching for. He looked at Tsurnick and noticed the Israeli captain had a pistol in his hand, as well. Tsurnick nodded and Bolan left the cage, knowing the Israeli would back his play.

The warrior raced to room 312, flattening himself against the wall as he tried the knob only to find it locked. The screams this time were definitely coming from inside the room. Flicking the 93-R into 3-shot mode, he aimed at the doorknob and squeezed the trigger. The 9 mm parabellum rounds shattered the lock and the door pushed open at Bolan's touch.

He swung the door wide and dropped to one knee as he leveled the Beretta before him. A man was trying to push the girl over the railing. Before the Executioner could issue a warning, the man's hand streaked for the gun in his shoulder holster.

Bolan squeezed the trigger of the Beretta, and the man's forehead dissolved into a crimson spray as the parabellums punched him over the railing. Then the warrior was a blur of motion, flinging himself across the room as the girl started a downward slide. Throwing himself headlong, he slid across the threshold of the balcony and slipped an arm through the railing to wrap around the girl's legs. He squeezed tightly, knowing his grip had to be causing her excruciating pain but not daring to release her.

"Tsurnick," Bolan called through gritted teeth. His face was pressed painfully into the railing and he felt blood run down his cheek. Dust from the balcony floor found its way into his nose, and he had to fight the urge to sneeze.

"Here," the Israeli answered.

Bolan felt the girl's weight reduced against his arm, then finally taken off. He got his feet under him and stood quickly to help Tsurnick pull the girl to safety.

"Who are you?" she asked dazedly as she was guided back into the hotel room.

"There's no time now, girl," the Israeli captain said.

Bolan silently agreed. The covers Mossad had arranged for the trip into Cairo would stand up under the scrutiny of airport officials, but never under a prolonged investigation that would arise if they were discovered in the hotel room with a dead man just below their balcony.

"But Constance was hurt," the girl protested.

"Where?" Bolan asked.

"Here," Tsurnick said as he knelt between the beds.

Bolan stepped forward until he could see the woman. She was lying on her side, her left arm covered with blood.

"Is she all right?" the girl asked.

"Yes," the Israeli replied. "The bullet passed through cleanly. She'll be okay."

"Get dressed," Bolan ordered gruffly, knowing the girl would remain frozen unless he made her move.

"But Constance..."

"Will be fine," Bolan said. "We won't be if the authorities find us here. And neither will you."

The girl nodded and moved toward the bathroom.

Bolan helped Tsurnick lift the injured woman to one of the beds. He made a compress from a pillowcase while the Israeli talked to the woman.

"How are you?" Tsurnick asked.

"Hurting. Is Krista here?"

"Yes, Constance, I'm all right," the girl said as she stepped from the bathroom and knelt by the bed.

Bolan pushed the compress onto the woman's shoulder and saw her flinch with pain. "Hold it firmly," he instructed, "until the doctor gets here."

The woman nodded her understanding.

"I wish I could stay until someone gets here," the girl said, "but I can't."

Constance touched the girl's face tenderly. "I understand, Krista. At least now you'll be in friendly hands." She looked at Bolan meaningfully.

The warrior nodded.

"My name," the girl said. "It isn't Krista. It's Helene. I didn't mean to lie to you, but it's been so long since I could trust anyone."

"I could tell."

Bolan took Helene by the shoulders and urged her to get to her feet. "We have to go."

"Thank you," Helene whispered to the woman. "I'm sorry you were hurt."

"I'll mend. You will, too."

"Keep the pressure on the compress," Bolan said as he followed Tsurnick and Helene. "We'll get a doctor in here as soon as we can."

The woman nodded.

"How badly are you injured?" Bolan asked when the elevator doors were closed.

"I think Konig broke my nose. I can't breathe through it." She snuffled and tears flowed from her open eye.

"Konig?"

"Yes. Eric Konig."

"Why was he trying to kill you?"

She raised her shoulders and dropped them, then glared at Bolan with her good eye. "Why does anyone try to kill anyone?"

"What does this picture mean to you?" Tsurnick asked, showing her the Polaroid.

"Nothing."

Knowing they would get nothing more out of her for the moment, Bolan remained quiet, hoping for an easy, unnoticed exit from the hotel. The elevator doors opened on the main lobby, and Tsurnick guided them out. Helene followed him closely, using his body to keep most people from seeing her.

Outside the building, they crowded into the waiting limousine, Helene between the two men.

"Look, Helene," Bolan said after the car slid into traffic, "I'm almost certain we're on your side in this thing. We're here in Cairo looking for Ris Thomas, and we know he's been turning this city upside down looking for you. What do you have that he wants?"

A sad smile lifted the corners of the girl's mouth, and her voice broke when she answered. "For the past eight months I've been his prisoner. He's held me in a small room and kept me for his sole pleasure. I've lost count of the times I've been raped. He only wants to possess me again."

"Why was Konig trying to kill you?"

"So I wouldn't stand in Ris's way of accomplishing the goal he was groomed for."

"How were you standing in the way?" Bolan asked. The girl had dropped into an almost trancelike state. Her voice was flat now, monotonic. He glanced at Tsurnick and saw that Tsurnick had noticed the change, as well. Bolan hated to push the girl after all she had evidently gone through, but they had to have answers.

"Because Ris wanted me. For some reason I seemed to become the only thing he ever wanted."

"What do you know of Phoenix Enterprises, Incorporated?"

"Ris and Kettwig run it."

"Where are they?"

"In the underground section of the building, I suppose."

"What is Ris's goal?"

"I'm not sure. It has something to do with the United States and the Soviet Union."

Irritation filled Bolan, and he wished the girl was more coherent. But then, if she was, maybe the answers wouldn't be coming at all. "Did you know Ris was connected to some kind of Nazi plot dating back to the Second World War?"

"Not until eight months ago," Helene said dully. "But never before then." Without warning she went limp and fell against Bolan's chest.

He caught her effortlessly, cradling her in his arms so that he could hear her breathing, wanting to make sure her broken nose wasn't still hemorrhaging down her throat. "What do you think?" he asked the Israeli.

"We're onto something, yes, but what? We still have no proof of any conspiracy against America and Russia. Even this girl's words may be the result of a delusion. And in her present shape, she might agree that Ris Thomas killed Anwar Sadat."

Bolan didn't say anything, feeling that in the end Tsurnick would take the situation at face value and authorize Israeli help. In his gut the Executioner knew he was right. And if he had to, Bolan figured he could blow the secret operation into the international headlines by himself. One way or another.

The limo's telephone rang, and Tsurnick picked it up. "It's for you." The Israeli extended the receiver.

"Striker?"

"Yeah, Jack."

"That historian you wanted to talk to has shown up. I've got him in our friends' airliner under wraps."

"Tell him I'm on my way."

"Roger."

"Has our hitchhiker put in an appearance yet?"

"Yes, and he's already been bitchin' about the coffee I make. He doesn't know how to appreciate it the way you do."

Bolan grinned. "Later, Jack."

The connection broke.

"Maybe we'll all know more in a few minutes," Bolan said as he handed the phone back. "The guy I mentioned has arrived."

"The man who explained the tattoo to you?"

"Yes."

"How would he know about this when the Allied forces knew nothing of it?"

Bolan stared at the Israeli captain levelly. "He wasn't on the Allied side."

Tsurnick's face hardened. "A Nazi. You didn't tell me we were going to be dealing with a Nazi."

"He's not a Nazi now," Bolan argued. "He was once a German soldier fighting for something he believed in, and he's perhaps the only resource we have for uncovering this operation.''

Tsurnick said nothing further, and Bolan wondered if the Mossad agents would be willing to put the events of the Holocaust behind them long enough to settle whatever menace lurked under Phoenix Enterprises.

13

"At the darkest hour of his life, Field Marshal Rommel called me," Joachim Koltzer said, "and revealed Wolfgang von Thoma's bizarre scheme." The old man sat in a folding chair in the Israeli hangar office surrounded by Mossad agents and told his story in unflinching detail. "As you know, Rommel committed suicide the following day at Hitler's request."

Bolan could feel the tension in the room, thick and electric. Turrin and Grimaldi took up wall space to his left, on either side of Helene, who sat spellbound in another folding chair. Tsurnick and eight of his men occupied the rest of the available space. Through the large plate-glass window overlooking the main hangar area, Bolan could see the bright afternoon sunlight glaring in through the open bays. The rest of Tsurnick's men were dressed in the appropriate airline coveralls, preparing for a fictional inspection they'd told the Egyptian air officials about.

Koltzer was rapier-thin with an erect carriage that was evident even when seated. Dressed as he was in a lightweight trench coat and inexpensive business suit, he looked ordinary, like someone you would barely glance at if you happened to pass him on the street. The fingers on his hands were almost fleshless, the right forefinger and thumb stained yellow from chain-smoking.

"What else can you tell us?" Tsurnick asked.

Bolan could hear the rancor in the Israeli's voice and knew Koltzer heard it, as well.

Koltzer gestured to the files Bolan had purchased from Faisal. "You already have all the hard evidence I have." He paused to light another cigarette from the butt of the first. "What you do not have is the supposition and guesswork I have accumulated over the past few decades. And it is still not much more than that."

"What happened to Wolfgang von Thoma?" Tsurnick asked.

"Sometime in the 1940s he became William Thomas, financial wizard."

"Why didn't you tell someone about this?" the Israeli captain asked.

A small smile flirted with Koltzer's thin lips. "Who was there to tell, Captain? The Nazi hunts after the war were every bit as bitter and vicious as the genocide of the Jews. Had I stepped forward I would have been found out, as well. I fought for my country during the war, and I am not afraid to say so."

"You're not now," Tsurnick said.

"Nor then." The man's gaze hardened. "But if I had come forward with the story I tell now, would anyone have listened, or would I have just been placed on trial with all the other Nazi war criminals?"

Tsurnick didn't back down from the other man's glare.

Koltzer looked back at Bolan. "There is not much else to tell, my friends. Over the years I heard small amounts of gossip, passed-on tales that this German scientist or that German military man had been recruited by von Thoma after the war, even shortly before. But I could not keep up with every move the man made. Von Thoma, or Thomas, was a clever man. He kept his interests diversified. Twice, I thought he had abandoned the building here in Cairo. Even our mutual friend had trouble tracking everything that transpired since the end of the war. I assumed von Thoma had given up his plans for any kind of world power play. The international scene had gotten too dangerous, too closed in to try any kind of coup without sacrificing millions of lives."

"But it was what he wanted," Helene offered.

Bolan looked at the girl.

She sat in the chair, not looking at any of them. Her fists were knotted in her lap.

"How do you know?" Bolan asked.

"I was there," she replied. "Ris told me about a lot of it. Thomas, von Thoma, whoever he really was, counted on a nuclear war between the United States and Russia to bring about Ragnarok, the Norse vision of the end of the world. He named the plan Ice Wolf."

"It fits," Koltzer said softly. "If you remember, gentlemen, Hitler tried to adopt the Norse gods and pantheon as the official religion of Germany. It suited his ideal of the perfect German soldier—blond hair, blue eyes, big men in stature. Wolfgang von Thoma possessed all of those. Judging from the madness Rommel said burned within the man, I can see him wanting to hold to those ideals."

"Ris told me," Helene said, "the plan was to wait until the United States and the Soviet Union started trying to make friendly overtures to each other, then kill the leaders of both countries at once, leaving them only each other to strike out at. There, in the underground complex of the Phoenix building, Ris and his men would be safe from the nuclear weapons, able to go out and rebuild whenever and wherever they wanted to."

"The underground complex can't be big enough to house enough people to make a stand in the carnage that would be left," Tsurnick said.

Helene looked up with tears in her eye. "Damn it, don't you understand? This is a madman's dream! Haven't you heard a word of what this man has been trying to tell you?" She pushed the tears away angrily. "The world may die in the next few hours while you sit here and worry whether or not it's possible."

"And Ris believes in the plans of his father?" Bolan asked.

"Ris doesn't think for himself." She looked away as if afraid to dredge up that part of her history. "From birth his father trained him to be everything his father ever wanted to be—a soldier, a leader. Those and more. He even had Ris help him commit suicide when he realized he wouldn't live to see Ice Wolf come true. Ris was sixteen years old. Can you imagine what that did to his mind?"

Bolan gave her a moment to regain her composure. He glanced at Koltzer with an upraised eyebrow. The German nodded. Tsurnick's face only held grim disbelief. A cold snake lay coiled in the pit of Bolan's stomach because he *did* believe. He had seen for himself the ravages of fanaticism in many different hellgrounds.

"I had heard that von Thoma sired two children," Koltzer said.

"No, just one."

"Ris?" Bolan asked.

"Yes, and he became everything his father wanted him to be. Even his name wasn't his own," Helene continued in a broken voice. "His given name is Fenris. His father named him after the Norse wolf-son of Loki. According to myth, the Fenris wolf will devour Odin and bring about the end of the world. That was the future Ris was given, and it was inscribed in the blood of his father.''

"How does Ris plan to set things in motion?" Bolan asked.

"By assassinating the American and Soviet leaders himself."

Bolan glanced at Grimaldi; the pilot nodded and left the room. If Phoenix Enterprises owned any planes at the airport, Grimaldi could find out quickly.

"And by using the satellite Phoenix Enterprises gave the Egyptians last year. It will interfere with the Star Wars program and the Russian equivalent to make it look as if both sides have started a nuclear war only hours after the assassinations. Ris has been in contact with a number of leaders of different movements whose ideals don't differ greatly from his own. He's using them all to achieve his goal. And there are more nuclear shelters around the world with factions of the Ice Wolf group who will follow Ris's lead. You've got to hurry. There can't be much time left." She looked imploringly at Bolan. "Please. I couldn't tell this to anyone before. I never had the chance. You've got to believe me!" She pointed at Koltzer. "You've heard what he's said and you know we haven't had time to make this up between ourselves."

"I believe you," Bolan said. He glanced at the Israeli captain and saw indecision on the man's face. "Coming?"

IN THE COCKPIT of the Israeli airliner, Bolan used the special frequency he had set up with Kurtzman before leaving the States. He recognized the Bear's voice at once. "Striker."

"Go, Striker." Kurtzman's voice was neutral.

"I need some intel, guy."

"Same file?"

"Yeah. I'm looking for a satellite that was given to the locals."

"By the parent company?"

"Yeah." Bolan glanced at Tsurnick, who sat in the pilot's seat, knowing the man's decision would be helped along by Kurtzman's answer. He knew the pressure the guy had to be operating under. Bolan usually ventured through his sorties solo, with a government that would deny his involvement. Tsurnick couldn't. If his involvement was found out, there would be vast international repercussions in this part of the world.

"Striker?"

"Yeah?"

"I found it. Awarded by PE, Inc., on March 6, 1982."

"How soon could we arrange a scrub on the bird?"

"It would be at least a couple of days before it could be done. And that's if you think we have enough factual evidence to convince the Department of Defense boys. Want me to get things rolling?"

"Negative. If it's going to be done on time, it looks like it's going to have to be down by ground control."

"Affirmative, Striker. Anything I can do from this end?"

"Wish me luck. Striker out." Bolan hung up the microphone and reached for the blueprints of the Phoenix building that had been included in Faisal's package. None of them showed the underground complex, but Bolan was able to put it together for himself after listening to Helene's description. "Are you with me?" he asked the Israeli. "If not, I'm going in alone to see how many rocks I can turn over and hope the Egyptians aren't slow on the uptake."

Tsurnick leaned forward to look over the blueprints. "We're with you."

"Thanks."

"Let's just hope we'll be in time," Tsurnick said. "How do you plan to get into the underground complex?"

"Consider what we're dealing with," Bolan said. "We have an underground complex that's prepared for an all-out nuclear war. They plan on shutting themselves off from the surface world, but they still have to have a source of power. They can't depend on batteries or any kind of stored energy. That'll be using too much power to imagine that any resource like that would be enough. But they're sitting next to a power supply that will run for centuries."

"The Nile," Tsurnick said.

Bolan traced the river beside the building with a fore-finger. "Exactly. And I'm willing to wager there's at least one water-powered generator concealed somewhere along that river wall. That's how we're getting in."

There was a knock on the cabin door, and Jack Grimaldi stuck his head in. "There was a plane owned by Phoenix Enterprises, Mack, but it took off three hours ago."

"Damn." Bolan checked his watch. There was still time to manage the hit-and-git strike and make it back to Washington before the meeting at the White House, but they'd be operating on tight numbers. He glanced back at the blueprints. He would call Brognola to warn him, fax a picture of Fenris Thomas and hope things turned out for the best, but he couldn't leave Egypt yet. No matter what, the threat of the killer satellite had to be taken out first.

Bolan moved, taking money from the ops fund aboard the airliner, mentally preparing a list of items for Turrin to purchase in the city. Scuba gear would be something Tsurnick's contacts wouldn't have on hand.

LEO TURRIN FLOATED easily under the surface of the river, watching the Executioner work. It amazed him how cool the man could be while working under pressure. This was Turrin's second tour along the river bottom. His hands were raw from pulling himself along the rough riverbed, searching for something that could be identified only as being something that didn't belong there. Hell, they were the ones that didn't belong. The little Fed was surprised none of the regular river traffic hadn't noticed them by now.

Glancing up, Turrin saw the dark shadow of the Israelis' rented boat hovering over his position like some protective storm cloud. He could tell from the darkening of the sky beyond the surface of the river that it would be dark soon, reminding him that an assassin was already stalking Washington, D.C.

He studied the bottom as he swam, conscious of the three other people covering the area, as well. He scanned the silt bed, which was covered with green broad-leaved plants he couldn't identify. Look for something that doesn't belong, Bolan had said. Everything Turrin saw seemed to have a specific place, from the plants to the worn-smooth surface of the riverbank to the silt that constantly shifted across the river bottom.

A shiny object caught his eye, and he changed course to intercept it. He floated, standing almost on his head, as he used his knife to pry the object loose. He wanted to curse when he found out it was just an empty can. He pitched the object away, watching it sparkle slowly through the river flow as the current carried it north to the Red Sea. Then just as suddenly it changed directions, breaking off at an angle to seek a new direction. For a moment the can rested against a lower portion of the riverbank before moving on.

Anticipation flared to life inside Turrin as he finned over to investigate. Looking for something that didn't belong, he almost missed something that *did* belong but was missing. As was the case with most of the river bottom, kelp and other plants lined the wall, hiding whatever natural nooks and crannies that had been formed by the wearing action of the river.

Puzzled, Turrin inspected the area. Everything seemed normal, until he noticed the absence of silt near the bottom of the rounded-out section of the riverbank. Grabbing fistfuls of the plants that lined the wall, he pulled himself downward to the base of the curvature. He felt his hair suctioned toward the bottom and stuck out a hand hesitantly, discovering that the worn planes of the riverbank formed a natural draw for the flow of the Nile. His fingers explored the lip of the eight-foot crevice that seemed lost in the river's darkness, coming to a stop against a fine mesh screen only a few inches inside the opening.

Pushing himself off the riverbank, Turrin swam against the current of the river, pulling himself through the water toward the Executioner.

BOLAN DREW A DIAGRAM on a sheet of paper so that the others crowded around him in the cabin of the small ship would understand better. "Whoever set this up has designed an airlock on the other side of the false wall of the riverbank," he said as he sketched. "But you can bet that's not the only fail-safe that was designed in the system. Without the air lock, the water-driven wheel wouldn't operate. The river wouldn't make it turn. But there has to be a set of emergency doors as well that can be shut in case something happens to the air lock. So we're going to plan on punching a hole through this wall and taking out their next line of defense."

"Won't the river follow us into the underground complex?" one of the Israelis asked.

Bolan nodded. "The underwater team is going to have a lot of factors to deal with at one time. We're going to have to blow our way inside to begin with, and navigate the suction of the river being pulled through the air lock. Once inside, we'll still be battling the rise of the water as it fills the complex and contending with an enemy force whose size we can't even guess at."

"Wouldn't the river take care of the viability of such a headquarters?" another man asked.

"Unless they've had other safety locks installed to compartmentalize the rest of the installation," Bolan answered.

"And then there's the wealth of information that's undoubtedly somewhere inside," Tsurnick said.

"Right," Bolan agreed. "If we can recover that, then maybe we can plug up some of the intelligence leaks in the United States and Russia. But most of all, I want to take this installation out. Any intelligence-gathering will be a plus." He watched the men nod in response. "This will be strictly an in-and-out operation, gentlemen, and it's going to be pure hell once we penetrate the perimeters of this thing. Our sole function as the underwater team is to blow up everything that gets in our way and head up through the building until we're on dry land again. The Egyptians can clean up the mess and sort through the rubble we leave."

"The land team will hit the front of the building at the same time the air lock is blown," Tsurnick said as he stepped forward to address his men. "Handle this as a civilian situation, because as far as we know, the businesses inside the building are legitimate. We want no innocent blood on our hands. Empty the offices as quickly as possible, securing the lower floor and blockading it immediately. According to the girl's story, the underwater team should be coming up through a false wall in the travel agency on the third floor. As they arrive you're to help with the wounded and get yourselves to the top of the building where the helicopters will rendezvous with us and transport us to the land vehicles, where we hope to lose radar detection. From there it should be a pleasant ride to the airport."

Bolan nodded at the Israeli and Tsurnick dismissed the men.

Tsurnick offered his hand. "I wish you luck with your mission, Mr. Bolan."

"And you with yours," Bolan replied as he took the hand. "Take care of Helene. We couldn't have gotten this far without her help, and Koltzer's."

Nodding, Tsurnick said, "Koltzer has already been escorted safely to his flight. I just hope it goes as well with our teams."

14

Bolan pressed the button on the detonator, and the false riverbank erupted. The water roiled around him, threatening to pull him from his position. Thick clods of dirt spun lazily through the water as a cloud of silt spumed outward, turning into an underwater fog that cut visibility dramatically.

The warrior flexed his legs and finned toward the underwater cave the explosives had created. The waterwheel had been blown from its moorings. Once he was in the new current, he didn't have to do more than guide himself through the opening.

Then the sensation switched from swimming to falling, and Bolan found himself on a concrete floor against a wall thirty feet from the aperture he'd created only seconds ago. Water continued to cascade into the enclosure, interrupted only by bodies that tumbled through the opening. Most of the men were washed up against the metal wall as he was, though some smashed painfully into the wreckage of the waterwheel to the right of the air lock.

Thumbing his flashlight to life, Bolan examined their surroundings. A metal wall barred their entrance into the complex.

The Executioner worked quickly, surveying the metal wall as the water rose to waist-level. He reached into the

underwater pack harnessed over his chest as he played the
flashlight over the seams of the metal wall. Choosing his
point, Bolan put down a line of C-4 and plugged in a
detonator.

"Down!" he yelled to the assembled men, waving in
case some of them couldn't hear him. Then he dived into
the rising water and triggered the detonator. The milling
water, suddenly released from its confines, raced in-
ward, no longer inhibited by the rising air pressure of the
air lock.

Bolan stumbled to his feet and kicked off his flippers.
He shrugged out of the air tanks as he crawled over the
ruin of the metal wall into the electrically lit corridor that
buzzed sporadically in front of his eyes. Evidently the
backup generators hadn't fully kicked in yet to compen-
sate for the loss of the water generator.

Clad in a lightweight blacksuit that fitted as snugly as
a second skin, and wearing black combat cosmetics tiger-
striped across his face, Bolan knew he wouldn't be easily
seen in the gloom. Fisting the Desert Eagle in one hand,
he removed a pair of black low-cut tennis shoes with the
other and slipped them on his feet. He glanced back to
make sure the rest of his team was doing the same.

As he positioned his combat harness around his
shoulders, Bolan saw a wavering figure running toward
them. For a moment he held his fire, wanting to make
sure in the uncertain light that the guy was one of the men
attached to the complex's security team. The bulky out-
line of the automatic rifle left no doubts at all, and the
Executioner fired two brainblasters into the man's forehead.

Grimly Bolan holstered the .44 in the combat rigging,
tying it down on his thigh. He took his lead weapon, an
Uzi, from the chest pack, then discarded the bag. Extra

clips for the weapons hung from waterproof bags at his waist.

Three men filled the opposite end of the hallway as Bolan and his men raced for it. Without breaking stride, the Executioner swept them away with a lethal figure eight of 9 mm parabellums.

Bolan paused at the corner, trying to get his bearings from the description of the complex that Helene had provided. The uncertain light made things a little more difficult because it was hard to judge distances in the long corridors.

The water had risen to Bolan's calves and showed no signs of slowing. There wouldn't be much time for any of them before the river swallowed the whole underground installation.

Bolan glanced over his shoulder and located Leo Turrin's grease-painted face, wanting to make sure the little Fed had made it this far. Turrin gave him a thumb's-up gesture and a tight smile.

"Did everyone make it?" Bolan asked the nearest Israeli.

"Yes."

Nodding, Bolan moved out again, motioning for the men to divide up on either side of the corridor as they claimed each foot of territory. At the end of the corridor they ran into a force of black-uniformed men who started shooting immediately.

Bolan whipped back behind the corner of the hallway as a line of bullets ripped through the dark water swirling around his legs. He heard a man next to him sigh softly as a bullet found its mark. Grabbing the man's belt, Bolan hauled him out of the water and back behind the safety of the hallway corner. A dark stain had spread down the man's left side.

"How bad is it?" Bolan asked as he helped the soldier to a standing position by the wall.

"I can walk."

"Good, because you're going to have to." Bolan reached inside the ammo bags at his waist and freed a grenade. He flipped the toggle and lobbed it toward his adversaries. He heard them yell, but their voices were drowned out by the immediate explosion. Water rushed back at Bolan's group, splashing from the walls and drenching them as the repercussion momentarily robbed them of their hearing. A miniature tidal wave swarmed through the confines of the hallway.

Bolan whirled around the corner as he lifted the Uzi to his hip. He emptied the magazine, blowing holes through the shadows that were trying to regain their balance on the wet and bloody concrete floor.

Another gunner raked a burst from around the corner at the intersection of the hallways. Bullets sparked from the concrete walls as they chopped after Bolan.

The Executioner dived into the murky, swirling water, keeping the Uzi dry as he landed on his elbows. He drew the drenched Desert Eagle from its holster and hammered a salvo of shots toward the exposed parts of the assassin, ripping the man free of the wall and flinging him outward.

Friendly fire raked over Bolan's head, stabbing into fresh arrivals who were about to open up on the Executioner. Pushing himself up, Bolan reloaded the .44 and the Uzi, dripping water as he surveyed the killzone. The smell of burned cordite stung his nose, and the deafness he was experiencing from the closed-in gunfire made a curious pressure on his eardrums.

It was slow going, Bolan thought as he led his troops through the concrete arteries leading to the heart of the decades-old Nazi scheme. But there was no turning back for Bolan or his men—they were pushed on by the inexorable rise of the river.

Bolan led the assault on the stairway leading to the second floor of the underground complex. Water was chest-high on most of the men now and the current that rushed through the corridors had become a life-threatening force. He emptied his last magazine for the Uzi at the three men attempting to hold the second-floor landing. Two of them fell over the railing into the dark waters lapping at the stairs, but the Uzi locked back empty before Bolan could bring it to bear on the third man.

Pitching himself to one side as he pushed himself up the stairs, Bolan drew the .44 and fired from the hip. The Nazi jerked in response as the 240-grain hollowpoints ripped through his chest cavity, then he slumped to the landing.

At the top of the stairs, Bolan had men toss grenades down both directions of the hallway, the ensuing explosions shaking the stairway. The warrior moved through the smoke-filled corridor, led by the Desert Eagle. The lighting wasn't any better at this level, but he could still see the two doorways on either side of the corridor and the blank wall at its end.

As he pressed forward, Bolan spotted the red lights of the security cameras monitoring the floor. He squeezed off single, carefully placed shots from the .44, exploding each camera in turn.

He had one of the Israelis attach a small charge of plastique to the door on the left, then had it blown off its hinges. Gunfire stabbed out of the room, bright orange flares that scraped sparks from the opposite wall, scattering concrete chips that stung Bolan's face and hands.

He laid a hand on the arm of an Israeli soldier who was about to lob a grenade inside. "Computer room. I don't want it destroyed unless absolutely necessary."

The man nodded and stepped back against the corridor wall.

Bolan moved down the wall, staying within what he assumed were the confines of the computer room. He indicated a portion of the wall to the explosives man. "I want a small hole here. I need the explosive to be inwardly directed so that it'll shove this section into the next room."

The soldier nodded and set about the task.

"I also want a charge placed at the doorway that'll go off only a second or two before this one goes."

"Yes, sir."

"Leo?"

"Yeah," Turrin replied, moving through the ranks.

Bolan noted the blood flowing from a cut over the Fed's right eye, but knew better than to acknowledge it at the moment. As long as Turrin was standing, he could be counted on. "Pick three men and cover that other door. There's no telling what'll happen when we invade this rat's nest. I don't want any surprises coming out of there until we're ready."

"You got it." Turrin made his selection and moved on.

"The water's at the top of the landing," one of the Israelis at the rear of the formation called.

"Doesn't leave us much time to secure the computer files," Bolan observed tersely. He looked at the explosives man. "Are you ready?"

The man nodded.

"I need this," Bolan said, indicating a Galil assault rifle one of the commandos was carrying. The soldier relinquished it immediately. After making sure the weapon had a full magazine, Bolan nodded to the demolitionist. Twin explosions, spaced a heartbeat apart, ripped through the corridor.

Bolan swiveled quickly, inserting the Galil into the hole that had been blown through the computer wall. He was aware of the savage gunfire that raked the corridor through the open doorway, because of the concrete chips that bounced off his back. No noise penetrated the ringing in his ears.

Five men were spaced behind various computer equipment and furniture in the large room. Evidently the computer room had its own backup generator, because the lights were much brighter in there. The hole was large enough to bring them all within striking range of the Galil.

Bolan squeezed off short bursts at each man. Only the last two knew exactly where the sniping was coming from, and neither had time to return fire or avoid the 7.62 mm hornets that ripped them into a black void.

"Goldstein," Bolan called. The computer expert Tsurnick had assigned to the underwater team came forward. "There's a phone in that room. Get that computer system on-line and plug it into the telephone connection. Dial this number. There's a guy waiting at the other end to copy everything we can transmit before the water damages the system."

Goldstein took the paper Bolan handed him. "I thought all American 555 numbers were false or for information purposes only."

Bolan grinned. "Not this one. At least not today."

The man nodded and vanished into the room.

Tossing the Galil back to the soldier he had borrowed it from, Bolan drew the Desert Eagle and came to a stop by Turrin. The lock on this door was different than the one on the computer room. Two .44 slugs smashed the mechanism, and the door pushed open gently.

The room was dark inside, but with his combat-enhanced night vision, Bolan could see the old man standing in the center of the room, resting heavily on the aluminum cane at his side.

Bolan kept his weapon aimed at the man and switched on the lights beside the doorway. He scanned the room and found it empty. There seemed to be other offices in the back, but he got the feeling no one was there.

"You're Fritz Kettwig?" Bolan asked.

The old German smiled. "Yes. I see my fame has preceded me. Just as yours has preceded you, Herr Belasko."

"You ordered the attacks on the people in the Witness Protection Program?" Turrin asked.

Bolan saw the taut mask of fury that stretched over the little Fed's face, softened somewhat by the false smile that turned up his lips.

"Yes," Kettwig admitted. "It was a good diversion for our ultimate plan."

"Those were innocent people, you coldhearted son of a bitch," Turrin grated in an icy voice.

"There are no innocents in war," Kettwig said simply. "Everyone is the enemy. If you don't believe me, check the history of your own country. Investigate the popular beliefs the Americans held about Germans in both World Wars, about the way they viewed the Vietnamese in that war. And ultimately, the view most of your country shares about the Russians that will eventually cause your downfall."

"You're wrong about that," Bolan said.

The German smiled. "Am I? Perhaps we'll all have a chance to find out before long."

"Where's Fenris Thomas?"

"Gone," Kettwig responded with a grim smile. "On a course with destiny. Just as we all are." He suddenly raised his right hand.

Bolan caught sight of the Luger and triggered the .44. Beside him, he heard the full-throated scream of Turrin's Uzi. The 9 mm parabellums turned Kettwig into a violently twisting mannequin before the body hit the floor.

Bolan stepped over the corpse and made his way to the offices in the back, investigating each in turn. The first was stark, barren. On the wall was a picture of two young men—one von Thoma?—wearing an Afrika Korps uniform and standing beside Rommel. Bolan recognized the famous general from books he'd read.

"Mack," Turrin called.

Bolan stepped away from the picture, aware of the spattering his shoes made on the floor. The water was still rising.

He found Turrin in another office, one where mustiness and the odor of age still clung to the walls. The office was a virtual treasure trove of German history of the Second World War: maps, books, pictures, models. All four walls were covered with memorabilia from that time period.

"What is it, Leo?" Bolan asked.

Wordlessly the little Fed handed over a framed picture.

Bolan accepted it, staring at the two children standing beside a seated Wolfgang von Thoma. A boy and a girl. Twins. His blood ran cold in his veins when he thought of the abuse Helene had suffered at the hand of Fenris Thomas.

"Koltzer was right," Turrin said. "There were two children."

"Yeah," Bolan said. "Were. Like Kettwig said, there were no innocents in the war they were planning. Not even the children of their own damn house."

"Sir?"

Bolan turned to face the Israeli soldier.

"Goldstein said to tell you the computer is burned out and that your friend was able to receive as much of the information as was possible."

"Good," Bolan said as he tried to clear the dark thoughts from his head, tried to forget the sixteen-year-old boy who had been forced to take his own father's life. Tried to forget the nightmare that had become the twin sister's life. He took the photograph from the glass frame and started to take it with him, then decided against it and left it on the desk. He knew the true story. That was enough. Let it die here and now with the history that had created it.

He followed Turrin and the Israeli soldier out of the office, moving across the flooded corridor to the small elevator that was conveying the team to the third floor. He stared through the closed doors at the carnage of von Thoma's mad dream. And this was only the start. The roots of the plot spread across the globe. Hopefully Kurtzman had pulled enough information from the files that would enable the different international agencies to trace the other people involved.

Tsurnick met him at the third floor. "We've got to hustle," he said as he jogged up the flight of stairs beside Bolan. "The Egyptians have already surrounded the base of the building and are battering down the barricades we erected."

"Did you lose anyone?" Bolan asked as they pushed through the emergency door.

Tsurnick nodded. "Two, but we brought them with us. And you?"

"Three, at last count, but we all came out together."

Tsurnick nodded grimly.

"Where's the girl?"

"In the helicopter with your pilot, Grimaldi."

"Is everything set up with the cars?"

"Yes."

Bolan nodded and climbed aboard the helicopter. Turrin was already inside and had assumed the shotgun seat beside Grimaldi. The seats had been torn out of the helicopters to make more room inside. Helene was sitting against the opposite wall of the open bay, hugging her knees to her chin as she cried silently.

She looked up as Bolan approached. "Is it over?" she asked in a broken voice.

Bolan sat beside her, not touching her, but wanting to offer solace and warmth just the same. "No," he replied. "Ris wasn't there."

Helene looked away, her shoulders shaking.

"Look," Bolan said gently, wishing he could make it easier for the girl. "I found a picture of both of you. I know. I also know that Ris told you a lot of things while he held you captive. I think he told you about what was going to happen in Washington, too."

The rotor overhead throbbed into quicker life.

"Helene, I need to know where Ris is."

The girl raised her head, the tears falling freely now. "Damn you! He's my brother! Don't you understand? For years I had been told he was dead. He was told I had died, murdered in one of the schools I attended. These lies were fabricated by our own father. If I hadn't gotten

suspicious of the 'inheritance' I kept receiving and followed it back to Cairo, I would never have seen him
again. None of this would have happened.''

"I know, Helene, and I wish I didn't have to ask you.
But so many lives hang in the balance now. He's not just
your brother. He's also what your father made him become.''

The helicopter lurched into the air suddenly, spilling
the girl into Bolan. She yelled in anger and beat at him
with both fists, almost toppling them through the open
bay of the helicopter.

Bolan held her tightly, aware that every face was on
them. He let her hit him, holding her firmly but not restraining her. Then, just as suddenly as the anger started,
it quit and she was sobbing against his shoulder, holding
on for comfort and security.

15

Ris slumped against the back wall of the pressroom, trying to appear as bored as the reporters surrounding him. The news conference with the American and Soviet leaders was already thirty minutes late. Was it because the two men wanted to keep their audience tense and eager, or did they suspect something?

The reporter standing next to him asked him for a cigarette. Ris looked at her as he rummaged in his jacket pocket for the pack of Marlboros he'd bought earlier.

"Thanks," the woman said gratefully. She had short blond hair that was cut straight across her forehead almost above her eyebrows. Her face was narrow, pinched, and she squinted often when she looked at the podium where the two leaders were to sit while answering the reporters' questions.

Ris put the pack away and turned his gaze, too, toward the podium with its myriad microphones. Memories of his father's words washed over him. What would the man say now, after seeing him this close to achieving the goal that had been set so long ago? Would there be pride in the wintery smile Ris remembered, or would it be nothing more than self-satisfaction?

"You're Gabe Hoban?" the woman asked, looking at the ID pin on his jacket.

"Yeah," Ris replied in a rough manner that was supposed to have ended further attempts at conversation. The shock of blond hair reminded him painfully of Helene.

"Lucy Crain," the reporter said as she stuck out her hand and named the paper she worked for. "This isn't your first time here, is it?"

Ris looked at her as he took the hand. Lucy stood well below his shoulder even though he slouched against the wall. Had he done something to give himself away?

The woman smiled at him. "I mean, you're so cool about everything, like you've got your mind on a zillion other things. Me, I've got goose bumps twice thinking about this."

He shifted against the wall and felt the reassuring weight of the SIG-Sauer in his jacket pocket, balanced by the heaviness of the two Misar MU-50 G hand grenades in the other. The jacket had been specially tailored to accommodate all of the items, just as the security man who planted the weapons on Ris when he was patted down at the door had been carefully selected to guard the pressroom at the White House that day. A lot of long-distance planning was paying off now, and Ris was surprised at the easiness of it.

The door near the podium opened abruptly and Secret Service men filed into the room, followed by the President and Gorbachev, who smiled and waved at the gathered reporters with practiced ease.

Ris felt a dark stirring at the back of his mind as something coldly familiar seemed to reach slick tentacles around him, through him, taking charge of his body. For a moment he seemed to linger outside of his body, almost large enough to fill the whole room by himself. Then he was trapped within the confines of flesh again, aware that his heart was thudding and his breathing had become more rapid.

"Damn it," Lucy Crain said as she stood on tiptoe, trying to see over the other reporters who had risen from their seats to honor the two world leaders. "We'll never be able to see a thing from here."

"It will open up in a few moments," Ris promised as he slid his hand around one of the spherical Misar grenades, tracing the toggle switch. He fisted the SIG-Sauer in his other hand. He'd pitch the grenade into the assembled reporters first to create confusion even as he was emptying the pistol's clip into the two leaders. Then he'd toss the second grenade up by the podium in case there were any survivors. If everything worked as planned, there would be enough confusion to permit him to leave the White House and board the federally marked helicopter that would land on the White House lawn for him. Once in the specially designed bunker only minutes outside of the Washington, D.C. area, he'd radio Kettwig and have the man signal the satellite. It would be Ragnarok within the hour. Even if Ris didn't survive the assassination attempt, Kettwig would trip the special frequencies. The world would die only to be reborn.

Just as his father had promised.

BOLAN RAN, pulling Helene along behind him as he followed the trio of Secret Service men down the halls of the White House to the pressroom. He knew from radio contact with Hal Brognola that the President and Gorbachev were already in the room.

He wished he didn't have to bring Helene along, didn't have to use her for the Judas goat he needed. But the warrior couldn't take the chance that Fenris Thomas had disguised himself somehow. Once Bolan showed up in the room, or anyone made the attempt to remove the President or Gorbachev, he knew that Fenris Thomas would explode into action.

He kept the Desert Eagle tucked in close to his body, holding it in his right hand under the jacket he'd borrowed from Grimaldi.

"I can't go on," Helene gasped.

Tightening his grip on her wrist, Bolan encouraged her. "You've got to. It's only a little farther." He looked ahead, watching as the three Secret Service men pushed people out of the way and waved others down.

"I'm going to be sick," Helene moaned, leaning into Bolan.

The girl's unexpected weight knocked the Executioner off stride, and he almost went down. His hand came from under the jacket with the .44 as he braced himself against the wall at his side. A woman behind him saw the gun and screamed.

Had the scream carried into the pressroom? Bolan wondered as he hid the Desert Eagle from view again and continued running. He wrapped his arm protectively over Helene's shoulders. Her breathing came in ragged gasps. They made another corner with Bolan almost carrying her.

Bolan looked at the side door that allowed the President to come and go freely from the pressroom. Brognola and Bowen, the CIA man, stood to one side.

A man separated himself from the crowd of Secret Service agents and flipped open an ID as he stepped in front of Bolan. "Harrigan," the man growled as he reached for Helene's arm, "head of the Secret Service. We'll take over now." The .45 in the agent's hand said he wasn't going to take no for an answer.

"Father?"

"Yes, Ris?"

"Did it hurt?"

"What?"

"Dying."

"Who's going to die?"

"I think maybe I will."

"Why do you think that?"

"I don't know."

"You're defeating yourself, boy."

"No."

"Yes. Never think of failure. Do you understand?"

"Yes, Father."

"If you do this, you will live forever."

"I know. You've told me."

"Now, come, boy. A pact. Between you and me."

"Not the knife, Father."

"Don't cry, Ris. Remember, this is your promise to me."

Ris pushed the dark voices back, tried to remember that all that had been said long ago. But it was coming true today. And he would do it. For his father.

He freed the grenade as he pulled the SIG-Sauer. Then the back door ripped open and drew his attention.

Without warning, Bowen stepped forward and kicked the Secret Service man in the crotch, dropping the man instantly. He lowered the little stuttergun to waist-level and held it on the other agents. Brognola backed his play at once.

"Go," Bowen said. "I know we've had our differences in the past, Belasko, but you've made a believer out of me. And this idiot isn't going to fuck things up now by staging a glory play."

Bolan didn't hesitate. He looked at Brognola, knowing his friend and the CIA section chief were placing their jobs and maybe their freedom on his ability to take out the assassin without anyone being hurt. He flattened against the wall, listening to someone introduce the President. It had to be now, and there was no margin for error. "Helene?"

She looked up at him, gave him a brief squeeze of reassurance, then nodded.

One shot.

Bolan opened the door, trying to shield Helene as much as he could from whatever possible danger was on the other side of the door. Surprised faces looked at him from the podium, and astonishment was written on every reporter's face that could see him. He searched the myriad faces hurriedly. Where was Ris?

One shot.

In another war one shot sometimes had cost him three or four days of hard work and penetration, as well as several lives. If a mission was scrubbed, it was carried out later. But there would be no "later" this time.

"There!" Helene shrilled in his ear, pointing.

Bolan swiveled his body, melding with his weapon, totally focusing on the one shot he would get before the press of reporters swept the big blond man who stood at the back from his view. He watched Ris's hands clear his jacket pockets, saw the pistol and grenade.

The .44 bucked against the Executioner's palm, the flat-nose hollowpoints ripping his target's face to bloody shreds. He held the pistol steady, at arm's length as he watched Ris Thomas fall to the floor, leaving a bloody shadow on the wall behind him.

Suddenly Helene was sobbing against his chest, reminding him that innocents were never safe in a mad-

man's war. And that was one thing Bolan fought for
every time he journeyed to the hellgrounds—the preser-
vation of the innocents from the savages. Even then, he
thought as he looked at Ris Thomas's corpse, no matter
how much blood a warrior shed, or how willing he was
to sacrifice himself for the cause, he couldn't save them
all.

The line between good and evil is a tightrope no man should walk. Unless that man is the Executioner.

BLOWOUT $3.95 ☐
Framed for murder and wanted by both sides of the law, Bolan
escapes into the icy German underground to stalk a Mafia-
protected drug baron.

TIGHTROPE $3.95 ☐
When top officials of international Intelligence agencies are
murdered, Mack Bolan pits his skill against an alliance of
renegade agents and uncovers a deadly scheme to murder the
U.S. President.

MOVING TARGET $3.95 ☐
America's most powerful corporations are reaping huge profits
by dealing in arms with anyone who can pay the price. Dogged
by assassins, Mack Bolan becomes caught in a power struggle
that might be his last.

FLESH & BLOOD $3.95 ☐
When Asian communities are victimized by predators among
their own—thriving gangs of smugglers, extortionists and
pimps—they turn to Mack Bolan for help.

Total Amount	$ _____
Plus 75¢ Postage	_____.75
Payment enclosed	$ _____

Please send a check or money order payable to Gold Eagle Books.

In the U.S.

Gold Eagle Books
901 Fuhrmann Blvd.
Box 1325
Buffalo, NY 14269-1325

In Canada

Gold Eagle Books
P.O. Box 609
Fort Erie, Ontario
L2A 5X3

Please Print

Name: _____

Address: _____

City: _____

State/Prov: _____

Zip/Postal Code: _____

SMB-3

by GAR WILSON

The battle-hardened five-man commando unit known as Phoenix Force continues its onslaught against the hard realities of global terrorism in an endless crusade for freedom, justice and the rights of the individual. Schooled in guerrilla warfare, equipped with the latest in lethal weapons, Phoenix Force's adventures have made them a legend in their own time. Phoenix Force is the free world's foreign legion!

"Gar Wilson is excellent! Raw action attacks the reader on every page."
—Don Pendleton

Phoenix Force titles are available wherever paperbacks are sold.

PF-1R

PHOENIX FORCE

GOLD
EAGLE

Take
4 explosive books
plus a
mystery bonus
FREE

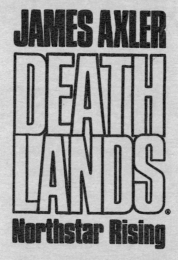